Acclaim for Chandani Lokugé

Praise for *Softly, as I leave you*

'… [a] poignant third novel … a must-read book.' – *Weekend Australian*

'Chandani Lokugé's literary style is drenched with powerful imagery, voluptuous description and acute observations of the fractured, uncertain nature of 21st century life. The heart-breaking clarity of her writing resonates long after reading …' – Susan Kurosawa

'The very language Chandani Lokugé's story is cast in – lyrical, wistful – shrouds the central character, Uma, in a mist of fine sensibilities … One of dream-like sensibilities … This is Melbourne-based Lokugé's fourth book of fiction, and, like her previous books, it is finely honed and softly written.' – *The Age*

'Very rarely does one encounter a contemporary novel in which the complex ethical and social concerns gradually fade away as the reader gets drawn in … At the beginning, we read the words of the monk: "Let go of the past and the future, and of the passions. […] Surrender to the present and that beautiful silence. Enter the purity of the lotus." This is exactly what *Softly, as I leave you* requires of the reader.' – *South Asian Review*

'A treacherous beauty pervades Chandani Lokugé's third novel, a tragic story of loss and squandered love … Lokugé's prose is filled with exquisite imagery and melancholy … Dreams and absences assume the place of genuine human bonds. The novel's message is a reproof to Keats – beauty is illusion, not truth at all.' – *Australian Book Review*

'The gut-wrenching loss of a child is imaginatively evoked' – *Transnational Literature*

Praise for *Turtle nest*

'poignant and beguiling.' – *The Age*

'a story of family secrets and illicit sex … told with such restraint and subtlety that it operates as a moving generational story of bereavement, desire and discovery …' – *Sydney Morning Herald*

'Lokugé's expert prose is drenched with imagery, the mood is hot and sea-salty, faintly threatening. We waft with Aruni day after seeming endless day as she delves further and further, scrap by tantalising scrap, into the truth. The powerful ending, at night, on the beach, amid sea-tossed coconuts with kernels "as soft as a woman's sex", is no less shocking for its inevitability.' – *Weekend Australian*

'a damning indictment of globalization's effects on local structures and environments in Sri Lanka.' – Anthony Carrigan, *Postcolonial Tourism: Literature, Culture and Environment*

'... [W]hat will persist in the memory are the characters and images, the beauty of the setting and the heartbreaking sadness of Mala's story.' – Writer's Radio, Radio Adelaide

'*Turtle nest* is a disturbing novel of great intensity and piercing pain ... [T]he quest for belonging is actually a warning of the dangers that accompany this quest.' – *Sunday Tribune*

Praise for *If the moon smiled*

'*If the moon smiled* is a poignant, painful tale of personal cataclysms and traumas; a tortuous journey of adjustments, tensions and human relationships within an emigrant family ... The writer's lyrical imagery is breathtaking ... Lokugé's words dance and cry in her pages ... *If the moon smiled* is a brooding, moody, nostalgic and haunting success.' – *Australian Financial Review*

'What a beautifully written, sad and touching story this is ... Lokugé writes with poise and a silk smooth touch.' – *Weekend Australian*

'The harsh psychological truths of this story are intertwined with Lokugé's use of the poetic language of Sri Lankan Buddhism. It movingly conveys the tragedy of the migrant generation their children's success stories leave behind.' – *The Bulletin*

'Original in conception, subtly ambiguous in its exploration of Manthri's emotional vulnerability, Chandani Lokugé's novel is heartbreakingly true to the inner lives of many Sri Lankan women "at home" and abroad.' – *Australian Book Review*

'Chandani Lokugé's haunting elegy for a particular kind of unexamined life, is moving, unsettling and unfailingly attractive. The writing is consistently beautiful...' – *Sunday Times*

'The enduring quality of the novel is its refined understanding and sensitive portrayal of intense emotion.' – *Canberra Sunday Times*

'*If the moon smiled* raises important questions: What does it mean when women writers denounce the traumatic experience of subjugation and sexual assault undergone by other women? What is the connection between individual psychic trauma and cultural representations of it? Is it possible to offer a textual/literary representation of trauma and to break the self-destructive patterns that rule most patriarchal societies?' – *South Asian Review*

Praise for *Moth and other stories*

'The world of Chandani Lokugé's short stories is a deceptive and deeply moving blend of the calm and the violent, the sensuous and the sinister. These are powerful, passionate, skillfully crafted stories in which ordinary people struggle to make their lives against the odds.' – Brian Matthews

'These are powerful short tales of life in a society under terrible stress – of betrayal, shame, unbearable debt, lovelessness, violence and even murder. It is dark hued writing but not somehow depressing to read.' – Robert Dessaix

'... provides a remarkably comprehensive insight ... into the subjective lives of Sri Lankan women and men, and thereby into a society under political stress. The double interactive trauma resulting from civil war, and the dehumanizing war games played within family and sexual circles, gives these stories a stark depth of feeling; a disconcerting justification of despair.' – Syd C. Harrex

'These stories show deep sensitivity and insight and are relevant not only to the people of Sri Lanka but to so many people today who are trapped by the few in a dehumanizing struggle for power.' – David Dabydeen

If the moon smiled

Also by Chandani Lokugé

Moth and other stories
Turtle nest
Softly, as I leave you

If the moon smiled

CHANDANI LOKUGÉ

ARCADIA

© Chandani Lokugé 2017

Published 2017 by ARCADIA
the general books' imprint of
Australian Scholarly Publishing Pty Ltd
7 Lt Lothian St Nth, North Melbourne, Vic 3051

Tel: 03 9329 6963 / Fax: 03 9329 5452
enquiry@scholarly.info / www.scholarly.info

ISBN 978-1-925588-23-1

First published by Penguin Books Australia 2000

Cover design Wayne Saunders

For Alex,
Shaamini and Amaali

The wattle is in full golden blossom and the most beautiful thing in the garden just now. The araliya that I take so much more trouble with, that I have nurtured for years, has shed all its leaves. It is autumn. The ends of branches are pinched and black-scabbed.

In the wattle's haze, I see my father's village. There, the araliya is laden with succulent green leaves and clusters of white blossoms. It is poya day. My father wakes up early and stands under the tree with his long stick, plucking flowers for the temple. He permits no one to do it for him. I see him through the window from my bed. He twists a bunch with the hook at the end of the stick and lowers it. Then, carefully, so as not to damage the petals, he removes the flowers from the bunch, one by one, collecting them in a small rattan basket. He will not pick a single flower off the ground. They must not be contaminated with dust or dirt.

The little girl can no longer contain herself in bed. She rushes out of the house. She wants to be involved in this flower romance. She takes the basket from her father and arranges the flowers in an intricate design. She pauses often to caress her face with the white-gold petals, and feels them delicate against her skin.

The village temple is small and built in the centre of vast lands. Her father holds her hand and together they enter the temple ground. They leave their slippers in the crevice by the gate. The little girl digs her toes in the sand, relishing the tingle on her bare soles. Her father stops to talk to this person and that.

The chief monk drapes his yellow robe close around his body.

'Worship the sadu,' her father tells her. He is always mild and indulgent with her. He arranges the fly-away frill of her bodice neatly around her shoulders. She worships the robe, her palms pressed one against the other at her forehead.

At times the monk invites them to his deep, dark lounge. The little girl sits with her father on the mat, facing the monk who addresses them from the low couch. She regards the ornate brass vases, the paper flowers, the mats intricately stitched of colourful remnant cloth. The monk's voice is the drone of a large bee.

After a while, she gets bored and runs away to the olinda tree by the side wall. She picks up its tiny red and black seeds. When she returns home she will ask Thilakasiri to pierce them in a chain.

As her father is about to enter the main hall, he beckons to her and they walk in together.

The Buddha stands on a lotus. The little girl barely reaches up to the tips of the pink cement petals.

Even now, I am fascinated by the tall majestic statue of the Buddha.

'You must try to be like that nelum flower,' her father often says to her, pointing to it. 'Blossom free of the mud in which it is born, unsoiled by it.'

Together they lay their flowers at the foot of the Buddha. An old man bends over and sweeps the faded flowers into a basket to make room for the fresh ones. The little girl listens to her father chant into his folded palms. She blends her voice with his: 'As these flowers must fade, so must my body towards destruction go.' But even as she chants she turns her face towards the old trembling fingers collecting dead flowers. If she had her way, she would bless them with immortality.

Her father moves back and kneels with other devotees, his back against the wall. He touches his forehead to the floor. There is a grace about him. The child sits close to him, her legs crossed before her. Her gaze crawls up, up to the face of the Buddha. She half closes her eyes and tries to purse her lips like he does. The edges of her mouth tremble with the effort. She looks around at all the people and grows subdued in the quiet atmosphere. Old women sit around in white cloth and bodice. Their faces stamp on her memory. They look weary and resigned. Their lips move eternally in chant.

Later, she would recall their story: the futility of their search for detachment in a world that passionately demanded and offered attachment. But now, she accepts the scriptures without question and is made tranquil. She imitates the women. She closes her eyes and concentrates on breathing deeply, in and out, in and out. She begins to feel a lightness, as if she were being lifted out of her body.

On the way back, they stop at the tea boutique to buy some white tissue paper for Vesak lanterns. Later on, through the month, whenever Thilakasiri is free, he will sit in their inner courtyard whistling under his breath, cutting and pasting the paper on the old bamboo frames.

She sits beside him, helping him. As the darkness encroaches, she draws her low stool closer to him. His mind is on other things. In a little while, having washed the pots and pans, Karuna will come out of the kitchen wiping her hands on her cloth. As she crosses the courtyard, Thilakasiri will tease her in a low voice. The little girl seeks to respond to him as Karuna would, glancing at him under lowered lashes, a half-smile lurking somewhere in the eyes.

He passes her another square of paper. As she dips her finger in the paste, he swats a mosquito on her bare knee, and carefully wipes out the smudge of blood. Large moths rush around the lamp above them and, singeing their wings, flutter down into the basin of water. Stirred by their agony, she edges towards the basin and lifts one wingless moth onto her hand.

'Leave it, baba,' Thilakasiri tells her. 'Can you give it new wings?' And, lifting the basin, he splashes the water onto the cement beyond. The moths scatter away in all directions.

Vesak. After returning from the temple, the little girl lights the candles. Thilakasiri takes them one by one from her and fixes them to the crossbar at the base of the lanterns. With Karuna, he draws the lanterns high into the air.

The mother lantern has a long wavy tail and her four babies have short feathery ones. Up in the air, they sway to a languid rhythm and shed a magical radiance over the garden.

It always rains before Vesak. The garden is full of puddles of water that reflect the lanterns. The little girl is perched gleefully on the low verandah wall. There is a sudden gust of wind. The lanterns dance dangerously making a sara-sara sara-sara sound.

Breathlessly I watch. Any moment now, they might go up in flames. And if they did, my father would say: 'Did you see that, duwa? That is the impermanence of life. All is transitory,' and wipe my childish tears away.

But they don't burn up this year and settle back to their rustling. The wind drops. The little girl breathes again. Her mother comes out onto the verandah and stands by her. She is dressed in her white sari. She has spent all day in the temple hall observing ata-sil. The scents of the temple are still on her. She combs down the child's hair and replaits it.

In the long still evenings after these activities, they would recall to her the colourful stories from the scriptures. Yasodara is a specially loved tale.

'So Yasodara renounced the world when Siddhartha left her to seek enlightenment soon after the birth of their first child,' the mother would say. 'She robed herself in yellow and when she heard that her husband was taking only one meal a day, she also did the same. When she heard that he had given up all luxury, she did the same: she gave up garlands and scents. She refused to remarry. So virtuous was she. In the end she became a nun.'

The little girl would immediately imagine her father disappearing into the temple. She and her lonely mother would then shave their heads and take the robe. Drawing closer to her mother she clutches tightly the edge of her sari.

'And the Buddha said to the king: "Not only in this last birth, O King, but even in a previous birth, Yasodara protected me and was devoted and faithful to me".'

The mysteries of births and rebirths. Sacred marriages. A wife's devotion.

'Will I also be married like that, Amma?'

Her mother smiles and strokes her hair.

'Yes, Manthri, you will. And like a floral offering to a deity, you will blossom for your husband and derive value from him.'

Her father stretches out in his armchair. He puffs at his cigar. The smoke curls in the air, pungent and grey. They gaze into the evening, the three of them.

May it go on, life after life, birth after birth. This moment, this dream: this memory.

Another year. For weeks now, she has been heralding the April New Year, cupping her hands at her lips and imitating the koha's piercing call.

I smile in the remembering.

Harvest … the sky is gold dusted with the rising sun. With Karuna following just a step or two behind, the little girl skips away to the paddy fields. On the way, she lingers under a cadju tree to pick up the nuts that sporting bats have let drop the night before. Occasionally she picks a fleshy, unblemished cadju-puhulam.

She climbs into the tree and shakes the leaves, teasing the bats out of their upside-down dreams. She hangs from her knees from a low branch and swings down. Now she sees the world as bats would, if bats could see. She squeezes her eyes shut and flaps her arms up and down, up and down. Her short skirt falls around her, half hiding her face.

Karuna laughs. 'You must have been a bat in white knickers in your previous life, Manthri baba,' she chortles and then, suddenly alerted, holds out her arms for the child.

'If your mother saw you now, she'd be angry with me:

"Karuna, you foolish girl," she'd say. "Don't you know that girls should not be climbing trees?'"

The child jumps down immediately.

The terraced paddy fields are a golden ribbon without end, pleating and folding down the valley. The little girl's father and Thilakasiri are already organising the harvesters into lines.

Paddy sheaves swell and surge in the breeze. She bends down and plucks a few seeds, then husks out the tiny white grain of rice and bites on it. She looks on as Karuna wraps a colourful cloth around her old one to take her place in the fields.

The heat of the midday sun. High-pitched, the songs of the harvesters. Do you see how hundreds of little paddy birds wheel just out of reach for the gleaning?

From the bund, the little girl imitates the harvesters. She sings their song and, arching forward, clutches an imaginary sheaf with her left hand, swipes it with her paper scythe and, gracefully stretching up, tosses it over her shoulder. She remembers to wipe her brow. The women laugh and indulge her.

But she overhears their gossip. 'What a karma,' they mutter to one another, shifting their glances surreptitiously from her to her father, 'not to have a son to carry on his name and inherit his wealth. All this will belong to her husband one day, to an outsider . . .'

The child runs to her father and puts her hand in his. He looks down at her absently, kindly. She is saddened that he has no son. She has felt her mother's distress and understands that nothing and no one can compensate for that loss.

Towards noon, her mother walks down from the house with village women carrying reed baskets full of rice and dried fish curry, jak and sambal.

All is in excess.

The threshing begins in the warm nights. The kerosene oil lamps make a circle of light in the fields. The men guide the lazy buffaloes round and round the threshing floor. Their canes crack loud and rough against thick hides. The buffaloes moan now and then, and try to butt one another. Thilakasiri picks up a song. Someone leans against a coconut tree and plays a bamboo flute, holding it sideways against pursed lips.

In the chill of dawn
In the blur of grey morning mist
She turns drowsily and smiles in her sleep.

She runs to the far end of the garden.

The lake is a still-life reflection of pure and cloud-less sky, and trees that stretch lover-like to embrace the water. Scattered haphazardly at different heights, the lotuses lift their faces to the sky.

She wades into the water. The mud is squelchy between her toes. She moves in among the blossoms, and cradling her face in her hands, raises it towards the sun.

She would be a lotus. Which would she be – a pure white nelum or a blue manel?

But, do they talk together sometimes? Or kiss? Do they only meditate? They must get so lonely, as they reach alone into the great emptiness. She turns impatiently to touch, to smell, to see. She breaks off a blossom and breathes it. She brushes her lips on purplish-blue petal. Secretly, she touches the stamen with her tongue. She is aware of a luminous inward glow, of water stirring against thighs.

A young man wades in from the other side. He bends over the lotuses, seeking half-open buds to sell at the temple stall the next morning. Usually, she would call to him and together they would gather a bucket or two. Today, she just moves further and further in.

Smiling, not smiling.

She looks back often, but she does not return. With every experience we are reborn but something in us is lost in the rebirth.

S he must be fourteen years old. The water splashes around the bucket as her father draws it out of the well. She squats on the cement, her short cloth tucked above crescent breasts. He lifts the bucket over her head and tilts it. The water sparkles silver in the sun and she braces. She shrieks as the icy water cascades over her.

Her mother comes up from the kitchen area. 'Stop shouting, Manthri. Do girls scream like that?' But there is tenderness. 'Let her bathe in the bathroom, from now on,' she says. 'She is getting too big for being seen like this. We must begin to protect her.'

They are in agreement. Together they smile down at her. Her lips quiver with cold. She hears Thilakasiri's whistle. It floats over her like a kokila's song.

Even now, it still does. It coils against my breasts. I can't breathe. It slithers away. I wander in the nights looking for it but it recedes into the void.

Her mother wraps her close in a large rough towel that smells of the sun, and leads her back to the house.

Her father sends the bucket crashing down the well

again. It knocks hollow against the sides.

There is the clank of metal, the grind of rope on metal loop and, far away, the thud of the bucket hitting the water.

The sense of things ending and beginning.

She is by the river with Thilakasiri and Karuna. She clings to childhood, reluctant to let it go. Karuna is washing clothes at the river's edge. The water swirls about her legs as she bends over and presses a cloth against the black rock. Soapy water squishes out from all around it. Thilakasiri stands against a coconut tree and whistles as he winds a bit of string around the tail of a dragonfly. When the fly is firmly fastened, he gives the string to the girl. She loosens it and the fly rushes away, its tail caught tight at the end of the string. Its wings are gold tissue. Soon, the string stretches and she begins to run behind the fly . . .

I remember looking back, laughing.

A rush of wind in hair, crisp dry leaves under bare feet, and Thilakasiri's involuntary smile. Suddenly she wilts. She lets the dragonfly go. Thilakasiri comes running.

'What is the matter, Manthri baba? Has a thorn pricked your foot?' And, lifting her off the ground into his arms, he shouts to Karuna to run for help.

She clings to him as he hurries with her to the house.

'What's the matter? What's the matter? Shhh, don't

cry,' he croons.

Her arm stretches across his chest; her fingers clutch his shoulder. She can't control her tears. She can't tell him what's happening to her.

'Thilakasiri, the dragonfly flew away.'

'Don't cry, baba. I will tie you a thousand flies tomorrow.'

She tries to hide from him the blood stains on her skirt.

'Lie down, Manthri,' her mother instructs her. 'You must not be seen these days. Keep that window half closed, Karuna.'

Manthri stretches out in bed. She stares up at the rafters. A squirrel shrieks a grievance as it rushes across the tiles.

Her mind wanders away out of the room, where the sun spreads a humid heat. The earth lies fallow in the paddy fields, awaiting rain and seeds and rebirth. The water in the river has receded. The drought has hardened the riverbeds. She yearns to be out there, placing her small feet in mud-dried footprints, guessing who had been there before her.

She returns reluctantly to the room. Life is suddenly private, four walls and semi-darkness. She gazes into the mirror. Already a new life is stirring. She slides her hands over her body, seeking its shape, and savours its response to touch. Softly she draws her lips against the inner sides of her arms. She lifts her palms upwards along her neck.

In a clay pot, a coconut flower blossoms. Small hard buds cling to pale gold stems. She turns her eyes away. They hold secrets now.

She has seen no one but Karuna and her mother for four days. When she stands by the window, her mother is displeased and leads her back to bed. Restlessly, she moves towards the light.

She sees Thilakasiri through the half-closed window vigorously rubbing his chest with a cloth. He has just bathed in the river and his hair gleams in the sun like melted tar. She calls to him in a low voice. He turns at once towards her room. He looks right and left furtively and hurries to her.

'Bring me some pera,' she commands him urgently. 'I will die of starvation on this diet of rice and pathola.'

Thilakasiri's laugh is soft and teasing.

'They are trying to turn you into a beautiful princess, baba, so that you will be a treasure for a king.' He melts away.

But later in the evening, he brings her the pera. She takes them through the window. He watches her bite into one, the flesh ripe and luscious, green on the outside, red-pink within. She runs her tongue over wet lips, dripping juice.

'Tell no one about this,' says Thilakasiri half in jest, 'or I will be tied to a tree and whipped.'

'I will be out of this room tomorrow. Will you tie up another dragonfly and keep it ready for me, for the afternoon?' she asks him.

But he is older than she, and wiser. He must have been twenty years old even then.

'You are not a child any more, baba, and will have to learn to cook and sew and get ready for marriage. There will be no more dragonflies.'

I wonder now whether there was regret in his voice. I don't remember. But, my world oozed like the milky sap of the jak tree.

Thilakasiri was right. She is not allowed down by the river with him any more and has to doze in the sultry afternoons like her mother.

But that's later, after her auspicious entrance into womanhood. After she has been ceremoniously cleansed of her impurities. After she has been formally led out of her room by her women attendants.

She sees her father standing by, awaiting her. She makes to run to him, in the old familiar way, but her mother holds her back with a slight frown and whispers to her. Made suddenly self-conscious, she shyly bows low at his feet, with her palms clasped. Solemnly, he lifts her up by her shoulders and clasps a gold chain round her neck. She smells the starch of his coat, and cigars. She would wrap her arms around his neck but restrains herself. He slides two gold bangles onto her arms. They welt her skin as he pushes them over her wrists. Then he returns her to the women, and turns away.

There is a pause in the evening's celebrations held in her honour. Seeing her alone, leaning over the low verandah wall, Thilakasiri approaches her. He greets her formally: 'Punchi menike.'

As if she had been waiting all her life for his words, she turns sideways, smiles, and enters his adult world. She glows preciously in this moment, his farewell to her childhood. And he, with reluctant, secret fingers, untangles a strand of her hair from the tulle frill of her bodice.

In this mercurial moment, a new ache begins.

But he does not linger. As she watches him walk quickly away, she hears Karuna's malicious giggle from behind the trees: 'Keep your eyes on the cows, Thilaké. Who are we to ride white horses?'

In the next year, she is boarded in a Buddhist girls' school in Colombo. Her parents would have her improve her English and learn social graces for a few years before they give her in marriage.

School. A heap of books. Bells. English tuition, especially for her, only for her. But it nurtures her love of books. In a bewildering nightmare, she is a faceless Maggie Tulliver wandering the lost tracks of the Red Deeps searching for two faceless lovers. She awakens to find that both are lost to her.

Colombo. She has seen it only from the distance before, on an occasional visit with her father, in a swirl of colour and noise, and change. Now, she visits it during weekends, with relatives. Parks and museums, the zoo and the cinema. In *My Fair Lady*, a beautiful flower girl's soul is reborn in the body of an unhappy princess ...

Traffic and crowds. People without faces elbowing past, in and out of oblivion. The sea. She sits on a rock on the beach and knots a wish into her handkerchief as the sun drowns in the sea. The beach is full of footprints. She tests them for size, wondering who had been, before her.

Lonely girl who could never get used to being away from home. Village girl, do you see how forest flowers droop on their stems now you have gone away?

In the early morning she gazes out of the dormitory windows. She spies a child running along the bunds of the paddy field flying a kite that Thilakasiri has constructed for her. He has made the kite to resemble her – a face with huge black eyes, a crescent-moon smile and two long black plaits with red paper-ribboned ends floating happily in the air. With his palm over her small fist, he guides the kite until it rushes into the blazing blue sky.

She turns away, opens a book and seeks to make friends with the people between the pages.

Days drag into weeks, and weeks into months and years. Long-awaited holidays fly past in an hour, and she is back in the detested school.

She absorbs herself in *Viragaya*. Why, she asks her literature teacher, did Aravinda so passively permit both women who loved and desired him to wander away to others?

'Ah,' the teacher pauses in her reading. 'You are too young to understand just now, Manthri. He loved both of them with a love that was removed from worldly desires. He demanded nothing at all in return, so he let them go.'

She knows about detachment. Yet, it had been reserved for the temple and the dhamma school. Never to be put into practice.

'But he was unhappy. And so were they. What was the point of it?'

'It was the birth of a higher truth for him, Manthri. In the end, the contentment that he attained from that detachment far exceeded anything he could have found in his attachment to the world. Read the scriptures again,' the teacher smiles tolerantly, 'and apply them to life.'

She rereads the familiar scriptures and recognises the truth of the teacher's words. But she cannot agree with it. Not just yet. Perhaps not ever.

The evenings are long, so very long. And then she is back among the changeless trees lining the banks of the lapping river. A kokila sings in the emerald leaves, and she turns to find his face. His voice seeps into her trembling soul. Her lips half part. She tastes the sweetness of his song and traps it in. She wades into the sunset where the nectar-filled lotuses fold up their petals for the night.

Lovingly, she turns the yellowed pages of an old book, the skeleton of a bo leaf pressed within them. The faint aroma of that other life wafts her back to the village temple where the camphor and sandalwood burn. Her mother lets her touch a fresh white wick to a flame sputtering on charred remains in a little clay lamp. In a moment, it begins to burn.

The same, yet not the same, her mother says. Like a soul dying in one life and being reborn into another.

She has returned home at last, a maiden, in an uncertain mood. She crosses the courtyard to the kitchen.

In its gloomy depths old Dingiri-Aachi is splitting a coconut.

'Come here, Manthri menike,' Dingiri says to her. 'Hold out your hands for some sweet coconut water.'

The old woman pulls the two halves of the coconut slightly apart so that the liquid pours into the delicately cupped hands. The maiden touches her lips to her palms and drinks. She raises her face to drain the liquid and a thin stream escapes down her chin, down her neck and seeps between her breasts.

The coconut falls apart in Dingiri's hands, exposing succulent kernels, and a plant just beginning to grow.

'Look, my menike, this is how you will be a few months after your wedding.' Dingiri's old face wrinkles up.

The maiden takes the half-coconut and cradles it. Her mother looks in her direction. 'Yes,' she says, prising apart the intimacy, 'she comes from a fertile family. Her horoscope predicts a son. It will be a fortunate marriage for her.'

Dingiri giggles and her loose front teeth flap. She touches the loved face and removes the coconut from reluctant hands.

'Come, come,' the mother admonishes. 'We don't have the whole day to spend in chatter. Have you arranged with the women to come in about a week before the wedding, Dingiri? There will be enough work to do.'

'Yes,' Dingiri chuckles noisily. 'We will work *before* the wedding. *After* the wedding it will be Manthri menike who will bear the burden.'

The mother chooses not to understand the insinuation. Sometimes Dingiri forgot that she was only a servant.

They get busy then, measuring the rice and discussing the menu for the night meal. The maiden moves to the window, and outside the sun is setting. The thambili tree bears great bunches of fruit. A village woman sits under it plaiting a coconut frond to thatch the roof of the granary. She wears a red bodice and, as she raises her fingers to her forehead to wipe off the sweat, you can see damp spots under her armpits. She looks up to smile.

The maiden is touched with a kind of tenderness. Home, where they know her and love her.

She turns back to the grating of the coconut in Dingiri-Aachi's hands. She picks up a few shreds from the nabiliya and tastes milk.

It seems she cannot be still, and moves to the soot-layered hearth. In its depth the fire smoulders. She leans over and stirs up the embers. Flames are lazy tongues licking the red-black coal.

She walks out of the kitchen and leans against the pillar just outside. She plays with her hair, twisting long strands around her finger.

Crows against the crimson sun. In the distance, temple bells. Richly, the evening sighs.

Thilakasiri is strolling up with Karuna from the banks of the river. Karuna sways her hips as she walks and wipes her wet hair with a towel. She smiles at Thilakasiri with the corners of eyes. He is whispering to her in a low voice.

The maiden observes them, still leaning languidly against the pillar. They see her and hurry up. Thilakasiri removes the handkerchief from his forehead. Twisting her wet hair into a kondé, Karuna hastens past into the kitchen.

'Manthri menike,' Thilakasiri greets the maiden affectionately. 'Can I cut you a thambili before I go? Or bring you a handful of ripe dam? We see you so rarely now.'

She is aware that her smile is spilling over. Thilakasiri is almost a stranger to her these days, but there is the bond of adolescent memory. The familiarity is tangible.

'What were you saying to Karuna that she must be so coy?' she laughs up at him.

She sees her face, and the evening's glow, in his eyes.

'I asked her to come down to the river with me this evening when she finishes the kitchen work,' he says.

She flushes with embarrassment. It was unlike him to be so disrespectful. She should snub him now and walk away with dignity. As her mother would. But, in his eyes: a lavish invitation.

Perhaps it was the way she stood there, her hair undone?

She is aware of ripening in the warm suspended moment.

Her mother walks out of the kitchen.

'Manthri, go in and plait your hair. It is almost sundown,' she says in a voice suddenly sharpened.

Thilakasiri greets her respectfully. She crisply orders him to tether the cows in the shed for the night.

The maiden leaves them. As she turns in at the courtyard towards her room, she looks back. There is no one by the pillar any more. She walks quickly away.

She hides a restless embryo, that night. Drums throb in the distance. Somewhere in the village an all-night exorcist ceremony is on. She pushes open the windows to an excess of moonlight. Moths brush her arms and flutter out of sight. She seeks silhouettes: Thilakasiri is with Karuna by the river bank. She listens to the swish-swish of waves caressing the banks. Karuna's face is thrown back, inviting embrace. They slide down together and now there is nothing to see but the full moon shedding silver on black.

The drums pulse. The exorcist is driving out the demon from a woman possessed. Coconuts dash, spitting fragments of white kernel. She should not stand alone here, by the open window. She must call Dingiri and ask her to sleep in the room with her. But she has delayed too long. Even as she turns, her shadow leaps on the wall, fearfully elongated. It commands and controls. It sways discordantly in the fierce conglomeration of sounds. The blood throbs. The demon shrieks out of the tormented woman. A severed branch crashes against the ground. In excruciating pain, she bears down.

The phantom rips free and rushes with streaming hair towards the river. She glows luminously between trees. Thilakasiri's voice hovers over her. 'I have brought you dam fruit,' he whispers. She reaches for the dam and is swept into his embrace. Her body responds endlessly to his. The arched neck, the curved lifted breast.

The river surges and soaks the banks. Surges and soaks the banks.

She leaves the window. She lies down in bed as in languorous afterbirth. The net falls, diaphanous and pale, around the bed, half hiding her.

Dawn breaks. Dingiri rushes in to tell her that both Thilakasiri and Karuna are missing. She takes the news calmly. The day's routine continues undisturbed. Another village woman takes Karuna's place. Thilakasiri is not replaced.

Soon, it is time to go into the shrine room. She pleads an excuse. She tells her mother that she is unwell and walks towards the river.

They have left no trace. She leans against a tree. There is only a vast spreading emptiness. And the fear that she will not forget.

It is the night before her wedding. I think she dreams. Her mother sits with her. The room is cavernous and floats in silvery light. Their eyes stray to the brilliant full moon.

'Vana Mohini must be on the prowl tonight,' her mother says.

The bride moves to the window. She searches the wilderness and sees the phantom she-demon standing by the river, lonely and beautiful, clutching to herself an infant. Her hair spreads and swirls behind her. Her body is touched with the chill glittering moon.

'Guard your husband from her, always, Manthri. Let her not lure him to destruction.'

'He will never know her,' the bride promises her mother from the depths of dream. 'I will protect him always from her, as you have instructed me, Amma.'

They pull the windows shut.

M ahendra sits on the balcony, reluctant to go in. The beach is deserted but for a woman or child drifting home. He watches the boats push through waves. Soon he can hardly distinguish their shapes. Only dim lanterns bobbing up and down, up and down, mark their existence.

He orders in brandy, coffee for her.

His eyes focus on the lights in the sea but stray back to her body. A bridal flower is caught in her hair, and a speck of confetti. The breeze disturbs her sari lying transparently on the rise of her breasts. He stumbles around memories of women in literature, and likens her breasts classically to swans. To clustering asoka blossoms trembling with the humming of bees.

The coffee goes cold in her cup.

He thinks of tomorrow with relief. Anything that happened tomorrow would be an improvement on tonight. He retires at last to bed. His new sarong is stiff. He removes his shirt. The night is humid and unfamiliar.

He speculates. He would be kind, and indulgent of her fears. He is pleased with her shyness. She had hardly talked to him during the day. That was fitting and expected.

He is tortured by her beauty. Now, his to touch, his to feel. Wife. Woman. He had only read of women's breasts, and thighs that could melt . . . like clouds.

His breath turns harsh and deep. Hearing it, he pulls back, ashamed. These were surely not the thoughts of a decent man. Up until now, he had only felt a distant kind of sympathy for all women with their inferior birth, their child-bearing. He wishes himself back in his narrow bed at home.

As he turns on his side she comes in from the bathroom. Alarmed, he half sits up. She turns to the dressing-table and he sees her like flames in the triple mirror, each one rising from a greater depth until the room burns with her. She raises her arm to brush her hair and he sees her armpit and, again, the swan-like curve of her breast. Her body rises and falls. Pauses and falls. Her hair cascades in tantalising waves and, in the swing of her hips, the fullness of her thighs, he scents a dangerous seductiveness. Watching her, he grows nervous and timid. Who else has he seen in the intimacy of a bedroom but his mother in her ruffled cotton housecoat?

He turns away, ashamed of her body, so much revealed. Uncertain of what to do, he switches off the light.

Darkness spreads like her hair across his face.

She lies down beside him. Her sigh passes him by to be recalled later. He turns at last to taste her breath and the silk-soft of her body. He welcomes the darkness and her passivity. This was how he had imagined it, if at all. With growing confidence he turns to her.

'What is it, Manthri? What is the matter? Are you afraid? I will not hurt you,' he murmurs. His nervous bird: his to feed and protect.

With inexpressible affection he draws her to him. He touches her forehead with his lips.

She is crying. He holds her awhile without speaking. Giving her time to settle down, to adjust. But she quivers and seems to relinquish herself where he cannot follow.

Something of his tender awakening collapses.

He would distastefully cast her aside, but shame drives him. The mocking lips of friends and relatives, and his right over her. He pauses until she quietens.

Only until she quietens.

Out of her silence she suddenly descends. She mourns and cleaves to him. A wantonness about her anguished cry, her intense gestures, arrests his desire. He will remember it always with shame. Had she no self-respect? No decency? She seemed a woman of endless wiles.

He will not be ensnared. He will not allow it. He pins

her down. He would strangle her very breathing.

Yet, he drowns in her.

Long stretch of silence, at last.

They turn to dress. He switches on the light. His eyes wander around the room, seeking solace.

The crushed white sheet bears no stain. He focuses on the cold centre of reason.

'You have been with another man?' he demands incredulously.

'No,' she cries. 'No,' but he flings the denial aside.

'She comes from a good conventional family,' his mother had persuaded him. 'A well-brought-up girl. She will be a pure, innocent wife.' His lips mockingly droop.

He walks out onto the balcony. He rests his arms on the rails. A lifetime passes. The moon is plunged in the sea. So all things must be: treacherous, illusory. White-edged waves smash against rocks, and fall back into water. They rise out of nothing and dissolve into nothing, losing their splendour in their insubstantiality. So all things must be. Slowly, he empties his mind of the dream of her. The salt wind stings his eyes.

Much later he returns to her and to, what seems to him, her endless delusion. In his tormented half-sleep he thinks he hears the echo of her footsteps, receding, receding. He will not wish them back.

A person driven by lust, he remembers, is like a spider caught and strangled in its own web.

But tonight, tomorrow, the night after, he will rise from their bed, obsessed by her treachery, by this woman to whom he has given his name, to whom he is bound by the shame of discovery. She who would bear his children.

She wraps her arms around her legs and coils tightly into herself.

'What are you hiding from me? Why did the family tell me nothing? How long have you known another man?'

She writhes to escape. She falls at his feet and pleads her innocence. He withdraws. She is not worthy of his touch.

His eyes probe and prod her body and he imagines, always, that it was her experience that he had sensed before.

She is a serpent slithering up from coils of serpents. He shoves her back into her cave of serpent bodies and scarlet tongues.

She stands at her mirror, draping around her a new sari. He regards her with cold, abasing eyes. As she sinks to the floor and into the flamboyant tangled silk, he pulls her up and pushes her against the bed.

There is a sense of worn-out triumph in him as she lies passive beneath him. And silent.

Afterwards, she reads late into the long airless nights. A bookmark falls out of the book. She picks it up, and glances at it in passing. Sigiri frescoes. Black-brown swirls the rock, and on it, golden-hued, half-veiled by mist, the radiance of women's painted bodies. Delicate blossoms unfold in slender hands. Inscribed below, a lonely wanderer's verse: *Dream-filled maidens, entwining a vatakolu flower with a blue katarolu flower, a golden one alongside one blue . . . I will remember you as evening falls.*

With lidless eyes, she seduces sleep. Later, in the fluid depths of darkness, the frescoes whisper their secrets. Figments of men's dreams are we, nothing but dreams, they say. Illusions, frescoes embracing rock, we hold not the power to disappoint, to hurt or be hurt.

At whose feet, the sleepless wanderer asks, do you lay your blossoms of gold and blue? Do you seek a secret lover, or merely worship dream?

Mutely, the maidens stare with their slanting lotus eyes, and lie against rock.

With lidless eyes, she seduces sleep. Let Mahendra be freed of hatred, and her of guilt.

As another dawn breaks, the child she was, the girl, the maiden, beckons her from the edges of life. She wishes she had spent more time with her, known her better. But she gave up somewhere along the way. She glimpses her now and then. A firefly, sparkling just out of reach.

And in the sight of this truth she is reborn as wife and, again, as mother.

So I transfer from my father's house into my husband's. I leave behind the temple, the river, the lotus lake. I write to my mother. In a postscript I ask her if Thilakasiri has returned. She writes back unhurriedly, distancing herself from my life.

> *Dingiri does not stop talking about you and the wedding. Everyone here says that the wedding was the grandest in the area for as long as they can remember. This pleases your father. He is busy these days. The paddy is about to be harvested.*
>
> *He is angry about Thilakasiri. You remember how he looked after everything for your father, employing people and all that. No, Thilakasiri has not returned. There is no trace of Karuna either. And after all that I have done for them. Karuna was a small child when she came to me, even before you were born. And Thilakasiri has been hang-*

ing around the house for as long as I can remember. Rotten, ungrateful people. Anyway, you wait and see. One day Karuna will turn up in rags and ask me to take her back. That devil Thilakasiri will leave her in a month or two. I know his kind. He must have already turned to other women. It is their bad karma. Oh yes.

Manthri, look after yourself. Convey our regards to Mahendra putha. Please come for a visit in the New Year. May the blessings of the Triple Gem shower on you. Your father thinks of you very often. He misses you always.

For months I scan the newspapers for reports of murders in my village. One day, without warning, the insurgency erupts in villages around the country. I seek the newspapers for the names of the leaders, captured and killed by the army. I hear of corpses of hundreds of young insurgents floating down the Kelani River. Was Thilakasiri among them?

I feel uneasy, something like guilt overwhelms, and draws sweat. I must extricate myself from the memory of a dream, I remind myself. I struggle to get more involved in the housework.

Mahendra returns home from work. I go out to the verandah to greet him. He looks through me. He walks straight
into the office room. I have placed his letters on his writing
table. He slits them with a letter opener, always from the left
to the right side. He blows into the envelope and pulls out
the sheet of paper within. He does not talk to me of its contents. I would like to know the writer of his letter – whoever
it was knew him better than I did. At least it was somebody
who could make him smile, a slight smile. I watch from the
outside. I move away.

I supervise the serving of dinner. We sit together at table. I dish out more curries for him. We are mostly silent as
we eat. He dips his fingers in the bowl of water placed on
his right-hand side and does not spill a drop as he rubs his
fingers together in it. He reaches for the serviette with his
left hand. Meticulously he wipes each finger of his right
hand. He lifts his chair slightly as he pushes it back. He
stands up and walks into the drawing room. I call Seela to
clear the table.

The newspapers are ready for him on the rack by his

chair. Later, he opens a file and checks numbers – dead black ants pasted neatly one below the other on white space. His pencil runs down vertically. It doesn't need to move diagonally. The lines never cross.

I turn the pages of my book of Jataka stories. There is nothing new in them. Suddenly I sense Mahendra's eyes. I see that the lungi cloth has parted slightly and my leg is exposed. Ashamed, I pull the cloth to conceal it. We go to bed about ten p.m.

I jolt awake to a chaotic silence. I am a dismembered body. Here a breast, there a floating thigh and swelling lip. I spin a web of desire to entrap the body parts, but they escape and connect high up where I can't reach.

I see her more sharply defined than myself: the lonely wild-eyed woman. I am nothing but phantom pain. The pain is intense. She slithers away, melts into walls.

My pillow has a lotus embroidered on it. Be like the nelum flower, my father said. Detached from life. Detached from desire.

In my dreams I construct a pyre. I extinguish the phantom woman. I would burn with her.

'We're going to Australia in January,' Mahendra announces. He looks around the table at the three of us.

'I've got a job contract in Adelaide.' His voice is curt and impatient, as if he wished to get this bit of information out of his way and attend to more serious matters.

'But, Mahendra, we can't just leave everything and go away. What about Amma and Appachi? What about? What about?'

'This is the thing with you. This is why I didn't tell you before. You'll always find something to protest about. What's wrong with leaving your parents for a few years? I'll be leaving my mother behind.'

'And the children. What about the children? And their schooling?'

'They'll benefit most of all. Aren't you sick of living in this small country like frogs in a well? No, I will open up the world for my son. Look here, Manthri, my mind is made up.'

'You'll like it in Australia,' Mahendra says to the children.

'Yes, yes, Australia. I know where it is on the world map. Come, malli, I'll show it to you. It's full of red deserts.' Nelum gets out of her chair excitedly. 'Can I tell all my friends about it?' she asks her father.

Three-year-old Devake has no idea what to make of it. He glances at his father and me with uncertain eyes. He follows his sister out of the room.

The rice cools on my plate. Mahendra continues to eat. I watch the methodical way he mixes curry with rice.

'Mahendra, this is our home. Why do you want us to go away?'

He places his plate aside. He dips his fingers in the finger bowl. He rises from his chair, then pushes it forward against the table.

'We have to move on. You always want everything to stay the way it is. I want more for me, more for my son. Australia is a land of opportunity. We might even migrate there if it works out.'

I gaze out of the window into the night. 'This must be my karma,' I say almost to myself.

Mahendra speaks to me from the widening distance: 'That's nonsense, Manthri. You talk like a village woman. We're only shown the path. We travel it our own way. We create our own karma.'

Later, seeing me still seated by the open window, he approaches me. 'They say Adelaide is like the hill country. You'll like it better than here. You never liked Colombo.' He lays his hand on my shoulder. Wordlessly, I bow my face to it.

Leaning forward, he shuts the window.

The keeper of the temple is a skeleton. It reminds one of the futility of attachment. The hermit monk meditates before the skeleton. His bones jut out of his body. As his hands lie lightly on his lap, one in the other, his fingers pass quietly over the beads of his rosary. His eyes are closed. It is only a body under the tree on the mat. The mind has escaped to course the noble truth.

I offer an almsgiving to the monks. Wherever one lives, one must struggle against attachment. That is the path to wisdom from ignorance.

I must free myself from the known and the loved, and bid farewell to my village, and my country. My mother organises a special pirith ceremony in the village home. I sit up all night listening to the chant of monks, but memories cling to the walls like cobwebs. My father sits by me, sorrowfully wishing me well. My mother hushes Devake to sleep on her lap. She sings an old lullaby that Karuna used to sing to me of a mother going a-milking and idly floating her pot of milk in the stream.

Towards dawn, my father ties a bit of sacred thread

around the wrist of each of us, for protection from the unknown.

One grey dawn in February, I gaze down from the clouds at the brown and green jigsaw puzzle of Australia. It seems complete without us. How will it fit us in? Would we be sawed into new shapes? I think of falling away to the surrounding emptiness: a being without centre or circumference, to disintegrate like ash in air.

The plane plummets, leaving behind sky and clouds. Devake holds out his arms. I return to the preordained.

With my two children clinging half asleep to me, I stand face to face with hot dry space. I turn round. I would lean against Mahendra. He places a hand, like a dead weight, on my shoulder. Then, bending down, he removes Devake's fingers from mine and takes possession of them. His eyes are focused on the distance.

'You have no choice,' my mother says to me. 'Your path now lies with your husband and children.'

I kneel down to touch my parents' feet in farewell. With the end of my sari, I wipe my tears away.

The taxi draws up. Nelum lets go of my hand and runs forward. Mahendra pulls her back.

I return from late-night shopping. Old Belair Road winds up the mountain. The car climbs effortlessly as from habit. It knows where I must go, has known for years now. As I swing from curve to curve, in the faraway suspended gloom the city trembles into light. I turn down the shutter for a breath of the eucalyptus of the hills, pure and piquant. The end of spring. Soon the skies will strip bare in the fierce heat of the summer, and wildflowers burn and wither in the valleys.

I park the car behind Mahendra's. I enter a dream, repeatedly dreamt on one visit to Sri Lanka.

Our house lies buried in semi-darkness in its splendid grove of gums. I listen, and the evening breathes. The grove lures me. I glide into it, and lie down in its embrace. I turn in the depths of it, sighing, like a woman loved and held.

In the lull, I open my eyes. Even as I do, the wind drives out the hushed calm. The gums close in, then recede, back and forth, back and forth. I wake up.

I stand at the entrance to my house.

Nelum helps me store away the weekly provisions. I

move listlessly. Late-night shopping wearies me so.

And it is, again, the beginning of a hot summer.

'Appachi is angry,' she tells me. 'Malli was practising his guitar and Appachi said stop it and go and study.'

'I should never have bought him that guitar,' I muse aloud in Sinhalese.

'No, Amma, it's cool. Appachi's just picking on him all the time.' She shrugs thin shoulders and takes the steps two at a time to her room.

They were growing up, my son and daughter. Soon they would start calling us Mum and Dad, and speak only in English. We were not equipped to deal with all that.

I look into Devake's room. He is hunched over his books. The guitar stands against his desk. Absently, he plucks at the strings. I close the door quietly.

Mahendra sits in the backyard outside the family room. The intense scent of the jasmine pervades. Further away, at the edge of the garden, the araliya blossoms at last. An Amaradeva lyric pours out into the night like a liquid dream.

I sit on the step at Mahendra's side, some distance away from him. The song and the scent of the jasmine stir in me a wistful yearning for home. The breath of a passing breeze brushes my bare arm. I raise my palm to my neck to wipe away the sweat. A childhood habit. But the skin is dry and hot.

Unaware of my presence, Mahendra sighs. I turn to look at him. As always he sits up very straight with his arms crossed on his chest. The garden lamp is aglow and highlights deep crevices on his face. Etched against the half-light, his profile broods. He sighs, yet again. The lyric, so mournful, so full of what we are, induces me to his side.

I lay my hand on his arm. Startled, he looks at it. And then down at me kneeling at his side. Our eyes bond in precious memory. He smiles sorrowfully. We listen together to the end of the song.

He touches my cheek and places his palm on my hand. 'Manthri,' he whispers as in a dream, 'my beautiful flower.' He bends to my face, to touch my lips to his. At once, I jolt back; my hand withdraws. I return to my earlier space. His eyes grow cold and mocking. His face hardens and sets. As before. As always.

Back home in Sri Lanka I've seen Thilakasiri set a match to a heap of dry leaves at the edge of our garden. As the flames blaze he pushes the leaves further into the burning core. Sparks fly up and drift in the darkness only to float down in disintegrating ash. Again and again, we are forced into the fire of our disharmony and relinquish our ashes to it.

Soon, without looking at me, Mahendra walks away into the house. I linger on. The cassette replays. And again replays. The music wraps lonely arms around me.

M ahendra has met a new migrant at the market and has invited him over to dinner. Just before the visitor arrives, Mahendra walks around the house, as always, inspecting everything. He walks into the lounge, first through the door leading in from the corridor, then through the door leading into the dining room. He stands in one particular spot towards the centre of the lounge and slowly turns round. He moves a stool slightly to the left. Everything must be symmetrical. Two massive brass vases, ornately inlaid with bronze and copper, stand exactly a foot away on either side of the kavichiya. The photographs on the piano have shifted in the dusting. He moves them into line. He surveys the mantelpiece and the large colourful batik wall hangings. He sees them to be impressive. No other Sri Lankan home could boast of so many local artefacts.

He walks into the kitchen where I am cooking. He looks in the saucepans and offers advice. One curry hasn't enough saffron in it, the other looks a bit watery.

Eagerly we embrace the functional.

'This Mr Gunasekera seems to be dying to eat some

rice and curry. I think we should put on a good show,' he says to me.

Everything is to his satisfaction tonight and he wipes his second-best crystal glasses for the visitor. The new migrant had not enjoyed too much imported luxury back in Sri Lanka, so what would be the point of parading the Stuart crystal before him? The cheaper stuff would impress him just the same.

Mahendra tells me that Mr Gunasekera has had some sort of clerical career, that he has lived in the outer suburbs of Colombo and that his children attended the less prestigious government schools. His family is still in Sri Lanka: he wants to gauge career opportunities before he brings them down. But how would he get a job? Mr Gunasekera speaks only broken English. Factory work, that would be his line. All this Mahendra notes with a satisfied air.

The new migrant arrives about half an hour after the appointed time. He does this deliberately. It would be demeaning to be at the doorstep sharp on time, as if he were starving and couldn't wait to gobble down his dinner. He rings the doorbell timidly. I see all this with my eyes closed. The tiled verandah is polished spotless and he looks worriedly at the trail of footprints that he has left behind. He hears the doorbell chime his arrival. He stands forlornly at the front door and wonders about the cost of the stained-glass in it. He traces one of the delicate panes of glass. A bird of paradise glows resplendent against his fingers.

Mahendra opens the door with a flourish that takes the new migrant completely by surprise.

'Ah, hallo. Come in, come in, Mr Gunasekera. This won't do. What is your first name? Here in Australia we are all on first-names basis. I am Mahendra and this is my wife, Manthri.'

'Lal, I am Lal, Mr, uh . . . Mahendra,' he says, smiling effusively.

Mahendra leads him down the corridor and into the lounge. I follow close behind.

Mahendra directs him to the sofa. 'Sit, sit, Lal,' he says.

Lal sits at the edge of our deep kavichiya with his hands clasped between his knees. He keeps rubbing his hands together as if to warm them. Mahendra sits down on a chair opposite and I rest on the edge of the piano stool. Mahendra does not make conversation for a minute or two. He lets it all sink in: the shining brass on the walls and on the carpet, the batiks, the chandelier. He looks around with pride.

'We like to have our own things around us, don't we?'

Quite overwhelmed, Lal gushes, 'Yes, yes, that is so,' to every question.

I look around the lounge and I see that it resembles a handcraft shop in Colombo. I am sure that our visitor swallows the thought for fear of giving offence.

'Have you met any other Sri Lankans?' Mahendra asks.

'No, no. You all are first,' he says, twisting his hands between his knees. He glances in my direction.

'Mr . . . Mahendra told me you came to Australia in 1980.'

'Yes,' I reply, switching to Sinhalese. 'It's almost twelve years now. But it seems longer. We came just for three years. And then . . . and then . . .'

'Then, the war began over there,' Mahendra takes over. 'So we went back and put in our migration papers. I already had a job in Adelaide, so it wasn't a problem.'

'The children's education, you know,' I add lamely.

'Ah, yes. It's always the children, isn't it? That's why I am also here. Education has gone to the dogs in Sri Lanka. There is no discipline. Schools and universities are closed most of the time. Terrorists everywhere. Landmines in Jaffna. Suicide bombers in Colombo. People dying like flies. What's the use of talking about it? You must be getting all the news from there . . . no? That's good. It worked out easy for you, but migration is very difficult these days. The paperwork takes a long long time, no? For me, it took one year.'

'The thing to do is to use a bit of pull,' Mahendra chuckles. 'It's easy if you know someone. Our papers came through in a week.'

Our visitor lowers his eyes.

Then, brightening up, he tries again. 'You are an accountant? You like your job?'

'Yes,' Mahendra replies shortly. The silence spreads.

A bit offhand now, Mahendra offers him a drink.

'Ah, anything, anything is all right. Doesn't matter,' Lal gushes.

'No, no. Tell me what you'd like. Whisky? Some sherry? Wine? Gin? What? What?'

'Anything. Whisky is good.'

'With ice? With soda?' Mahendra glances meaningfully in my direction.

Lal leans forward and takes the glass from Mahendra's hands in both of his. It throws shafts of coloured light. He takes a sip. It hits his empty stomach like fire. Tears spring into his eyes. Pretending to have seen nothing, Mahendra swirls his own drink expertly, making the ice cubes crackle.

Lal looks towards me like a dog about to be whipped.

'Take a few peanuts, Lal,' I say to him, softly.

He seems to read behind my eyes. He sees that all is not right in this opulence, and smiles with me distantly, but with something like compassion, the way the monk in our village temple would smile when speculating on human foibles.

He leans back against the kavichiya and looks towards Mahendra with more confidence.

I am ashamed of the exchange. I feel disloyal. As I turn round, I catch Mahendra's eyes. As always, the implication hurts.

'Do you work as well?' the visitor asks me.

'I wanted to . . .' I begin.

But Mahendra continues: 'Child care would have cost us much more than what she could have earned, and who can look after the children better than their mother? No, she has never worked,' he concludes with some pride.

I go in to organise dinner. Devake and Nelum are in the kitchen surreptitiously serving themselves, hoping to escape with their plates into the family room. I persuade Devake to join us at the formal table. Nelum refuses and settles down in front of the TV. As we eat, Devake tries to communicate nervously with Lal. They talk a bit about schools and exams. I sit by, mainly silent. Mahendra takes over often, controlling the conversation, making sure the right image is projected by all of us. As soon as dinner is over, Devake leaves the table.

Later, in our room, Mahendra accuses me of seducing our visitor. He reminds me of the past. His voice rasps terribly. Flushed and ashamed, I look away. As always.

'Don't raise your voice,' I plead with him at last. 'The children will hear you.'

As usual, I shake loose my hair for the night. I turn to the dressing-table for the brush. In the mirror, I see his eyes fixed on my body. My hair is long and falls down my back in thick coils. 'Come with me to the river,' Thilakasiri whispers to me. His face is closing in on me, like a face held too close to a camera, or to the truth.

I twist my hair tightly into a kondé.

I lie down in bed, next to Mahendra. It is his wish that I do not move, that I lie passive.

Outside, I hear the gums swinging back and forth, back and forth, now closing in, now receding. I change shape and form – first in the arms of a lover, and then of a husband.

Later that night, I bury my face in my pillow. Every breath I take is a sob. As of habit, I seek to blame someone. Had my horoscope lied? Had the astrologer mixed up my birth time with someone else's? What happiness had my parents shared when they arranged my marriage. With what pride had my father given me away to Mahendra.

Had I myself not been full of hope as a bride?

As the bridal drums throbbed and blessed water trickled over our two fingers bound together and touching one another for the first time, had I not vowed to be his devoted wife? Would I not be what my mother was to my father? Is it my karma that this cannot be?

It is strange that one's horoscope does not house joy in marriage. Your wedded life will steer towards fulfilment, it had predicted, with no mention of happiness. Well, I have been fulfilled. How else could a woman be fulfilled in marriage but with a son who would continue his father's name?

But joy eludes. It haunts the river banks where a phantom roams the moon-stained earth. I twist and turn, in the remembering. Perhaps, had I set flame to that night when the light of the full moon had drenched my maiden loins, and scattered the ash in the river, it would not claim me like this, time and time again.

Long ago, a dead woman floated down the river. I remember her eyes, wide open and staring into mine. They said she had been seduced by the full moon. As I bent over to look closer, Thilakasiri dragged me away from the banks, pressing his fingers against my eyes.

Now, I try to control my sobs and my mind's wanderings. Mahendra turns in his sleep and draws me towards him.

As I shut my eyes, I recall the scriptures. All pain is born of desire, of desire for one's own happiness. And samsara, after all, is a catharsis that leads to that luminous emptiness of absence of desire. Towards this end, must I strive.

The creek at the edge of our garden is parched and cracked. The land is dehydrating. There are warnings about bushfires. TV rekindles memories of Ash Wednesday, when birds and koalas burnt alive in trees. I could do with a walk, but we stay in because it is too hot to venture out.

The house is a sealed box, artificially cooled. Now here, now there, we walk around trying not to knock against each other. Mahendra sits in the family room. I wander in. He does not look up from the newspapers. I read a bit of my library book. The woman in the story realises love is an illusion but tries to cup it in her hands anyway. I will return the book on Friday and try another author. I would be in love with life itself.

I go in search of the children. Devake has shut himself up in his room. He is laughing into the telephone. What an infectious laugh he reserves for his friends. I walk into Nelum's room. She sits on her bed, sketching. I peer over her shoulder.

'I'll show it to you later, Mum,' she says impatiently, hiding the picture with her hands.

The paper is a swirl of colour. I can make out no design or figure. Why doesn't she draw something beautiful, like a lotus unfolding petal on velvet petal for the sun? But she doesn't know the lotus as I do, even though she is its manifestation. I move away from her, to stand at her window and gaze out.

A large magpie is perched on the empty birdbath. Poor thirsty bird. I carry a bucket of water out of the house. The heat is unbearable on the skin. As I approach the bath, the bird writhes spasmodically on the grass, squawking raucously. Even as I rush up to it, it dies.

There is the echo of a wild, reverberating shriek. Disturbed by my movements, Mahendra comes outside. He glances at the bird, and at me. I fear that he is about to make some sardonic comment. I try to mask my parched face.

'Go inside, Manthri,' he says. 'It is too hot for you. I'll bury the bird.'

I could fall at his feet in worship.

But he turns back to the house. Moments like this are brilliant drops of mirage rain.

The monk is Thai, benign and welcoming. The small temple fills with devotees on Vas and Vesak. There is no Sri Lankan temple in Adelaide and we share one with the Thai. I wish we lived in Melbourne where I could attend one of our own temples. But there is some talk that soon there will be our own temple in Adelaide. Perhaps then my mother and father would visit me. Thinking of my father, I walk round the bo sapling. I have heard that it is from Sri Lanka. It is shedding leaves. I pick up one or two to press between pages. The vine on the temple wall has turned scarlet.

There is a great deal of noise. Women and men and children weave in and out. Joss sticks send up tendrils of smoke. The chief monk addresses the crowd. He speaks of the familiar in an unfamiliar tongue. I am not accustomed to a Buddhist sermon preached in English by a Thai monk.

The monks are served rice with a variety of Sri Lankan and Thai curries, and soon after, we all share the remains. The curries do not seem to blend. The people are friendly and happy, greeting each other loudly and fondling children.

It is a day out for all of us. We have been looking forward to today. All are feeling meritorious having offered alms to the monks. The light autumn breeze coaxes us to linger on. Idly, we pick at strands of conversation.

'Ah, Manthri.' A small group of ladies suddenly becomes conscious of me. 'How, how? What news?'

I have no news. I smile. They ask me why my children are not here today.

Rita replies for me: 'They are busy, no? Even my two went off on a picnic early in the morning. What to do? Children grow up. We can't force them to do anything. Now, if it was back home, there would have been no question about it. We would tell them to get in the car, and they would get in the car, no?' She sighs nostalgically.

A few parents have brought their children to temple today. Their smiles reveal the effort of their small success. Still, there is some envy among us.

'I can't go, Mum,' Nelum said to me this morning. 'All those gossipy friends of yours will look me up and down and sideways. I have more interesting things to do.'

I return to the conversation, putting in a word absently. No one listens much to anyone. Sumana has an arresting bit of news about how Srimani's son has just got engaged to a wealthy girl back home. And after he had been carrying on with a Greek or Italian girl here in Adelaide for years. They cup their chins in their hands, reflecting. The things that happen.

'But what can you expect?' Rita justifies. 'We brought the children here, and exposed them to this life. How can we expect them to be Sri Lankan through and through?'

Prema suddenly turns on me. 'What's this about Devake?'

Her smile includes us all. I guess they have shared this bit of news before I arrived.

'Has he really shaved off all his hair? What does Mahendra think about it? When Rohan tried growing his hair in a ponytail, we told him we would have no such nonsense in our house. We have to preserve something of our culture, don't you think? Wherever we are? Without that we have nothing, no? Are you going to tolerate this, Manthri?'

They are greedy for developments. My smile must split my face. Their faces swing out of proportion. Lips swell and blab. I clutch the branch of a tree. I would die rather than break down.

Why can't I turn it into a joke? This is trivial, after all. Why must I be embittered and seek refuge? Mahendra would say that I am unsociable. I am. Always on the fringe, wanting to … only to surrender to an inexplicable isolation.

These are self-imposed bonds, the village monk would preach to me. I alone can extricate myself from my isolation and reach that tranquil state where I may torture myself no more.

Stirred by the breeze, dry leaves crackle around our feet. Whoever it was who thought of scattered dry leaves as coffins of little children thought right. I had felt the image morbid when I read it.

'The trees are shedding all their leaves. Don't you wish they'd stay fresh and green?' I look down embarrassed. How irrelevantly I speak.

They turn away with faintly veiled impatience and slightly mocking smiles. I walk in the direction of the shrine room. I feel their eyes drill holes in my head as they return to their gossip. To Mahendra, to Devake, to us. Oh yes, but they'd seen it coming all along. Devake had never been very promising anyway. Always hanging on to Manthri's sari. Mahendra of course has high hopes, they must be saying. Their voices whisper around me even when I sleep.

The shrine room is noisy with children running in and out. Women talk among themselves as they light joss sticks.

A dull headache begins to grow like a tumour.

The temple is emptying. I go in search of Mahendra. He's discussing the Sri Lankan war with the men. Children as young as eighteen are enlisting in the army. Someone is showing around *The Island* newspaper. I look in on graphic photographs of the headless corpse of a suicide bomber. Shredded limbs hang from trees. A village child stares wild-eyed at the severed head of her father. We are fortunate to be out of that bloody mess, Mahendra says loudly. Let us count our blessings. No one agrees or disagrees.

We would cover up the guilt, if we could. Someone suggests that we ship over our children's outgrown clothes to the war-torn villages. Another suggests donations and medical equipment.

I remember a Jataka story. A mendicant was starving to death in the forest one night. Seeing this, the Bodhisattva transformed into a hare which plunged its little body into the fire. Deeply moved by its generosity, the gods rescued it and engraved its form on the moon. To this day, we recall the story to our children back home, when we show them the hare on the full moon.

But now, wallowing in our luxuries, we try to salve our conscience by sacrificing our second-hand clothes and excess wealth. Without a word, I fall in with their plans.

Mahendra sees me at last.

'Shall we go?' I look at him with my pleading eyes. I know they are always pleading, irritating.

'Collect the dishes,' he says.

But Suranjith intervenes: 'We're all going to meet at Sumith's house after this. Drink some tea, sing a few songs. Like in those good old days. Won't you and Mahendra come along, Manthri? We don't see you much these days.' His voice is touched with friendliness. We had been friends, once.

Those long and wonderful evenings when we sang one Sinhala song after another.

I close my eyes. The children sit by my feet on the carpet. I listen to Mahendra's alluring voice and join in softly with a line now and then. Images contained within the lyrics take flight heartbreakingly, like flocks of white birds hovering over a sacred dagaba on a poya night. The sunset seeps through their wings and spreads a gentle lustre on the wind-lulled bo leaves in the temple grounds. In the far distance, carrying a sheaf of long-stemmed buds, a woman dressed all in white walks to temple along the bunds of the paddy fields.

A voice trembles with tears. Mahendra lays his arm around me.

Outside, the winter mists swirl into fog and naked branches knock against the windowpanes. Soon, they burst into glorious leaf in every shade of green. The evenings are longer and we sit out in the yards. Then, the leaves redden and the autumn chill settles in. We move back in and crowd by the fire.

One evening I look down, and the children no longer sit at my feet. They have not learnt to sing our songs.

But, I do not regret that we grew away. These simple evenings trailed poisoned gossip in their wake.

Mahendra no longer talks to Devake. Not only has Devake shaved his hair, he has also taken to some kind of drug. He comes in late and sometimes topples a chair or book. I rush up to his door. It is locked. I hear him in the toilet. He does not answer my knock on his door, or my whispered 'putha, putha'. Sometimes I sit in the corridor outside his room and wait for him to come out.

He did come out one night – or was it early morning? – and spoke to me. His eyes were glazed, his voice slurred. He lifted me to my feet and helped me back to bed. I laid my head against his shoulder.

'I must talk to you,' I said.

'Later,' he said, 'tomorrow,' and led me to my door with a fleeting tenderness.

I leant a moment longer against him, clinging to my son's caring.

But the next day he did not look at me, or talk to me. I went to him a number of times. I touched his hair from behind as he sat at his desk.

'Putha,' I said to him, 'I want to talk to you.'

'Not now, Mum. Not now. Leave me alone.'

He would not look at me. He shook his head away, impatiently. My hands fell back. He gripped the sides of the table, the edges of his fingers white. My tears wet his shirt.

'You have brought him up all wrong,' Mahendra says to me ten times a day. 'It is your job to bring up the children. Why can't you control them?'

Visitors ask: 'So what is Devake going to do at the university? He's sitting for his Matric this year, isn't he?' Devake's thin body stoops with the weight of the question. Mahendra replies in his stead, and Devake's hesitation is passed over.

'He's going to do medicine.'

Devake smiles and stammers. He knows, even as I do, that he will never get into medical school. Even some of our friends know. And they snigger a bit and ask: 'He will have to get a very high score, no? Devake, you'll have to try very hard.'

'Oh, no problem,' replies Mahendra for him. 'He will be fine. Won't you, Devake?' Won't you, Devake? Won't you, Devake?

Devake escapes to his room as quickly as possible. He sits at his table and presses his head between his hands, then jumps out of his chair and switches on the radio. He stares out of the window. The music carries him away. Suddenly he quivers back. Assignments to be completed. Mock exams next week. Feverishly he counts up the marks of his subjects. They don't add up to much. He organises a new revision timetable like Mahendra showed him. He slumps over it. It demands eight hours of his after-school day.

'I've sacrificed my whole life for you – my career, my country,' Mahendra dictates, 'only for you to have a good education. Go on, now, go and study. You must not neglect your work even for a moment.'

'Music? What music? What future with music, ah? Play in a band? Do you want the whole world to laugh at us? No, you're going to be a doctor. Go on, go on, don't sit there like a fool. Don't waste time. Go and start on your homework. I have arranged for you to have tuition in chemistry and maths.'

Devake lies down in bed, at last. He turns towards the wall and stares at nothing through empty eyes. In the depths of our nightmares, he gropes for my hand.

I glance at Nelum. She seems far away. She has cut herself out of it. Devake leaves the dining table. He climbs up the stairs, a step at a time. I rise in protest.

Mahendra gets up in disgust. 'Sit down, Manthri. You are the one who is spoiling him all the time. Let me handle him.'

I sit with Nelum.

'You and Dad are going to drive him mad,' she says, rising from her chair.

I linger at the table with the half-empty dishes.

I pluck at a grain of rice with my finger. I squash it against the plate. I stare at it. It is no longer a grain. It is a paste. I try to roll it back into shape. Am I going mad?

At home the paddy would be ripe for harvest now, and my mother would be getting the loft cleaned for sacks and sacks of grain. There would be a smile on my father's face. The smile warms my memory.

I have talked to no one today. I reflect on people I know. I go over conversations that I have absorbed on visits, an unguarded look on the face of an acquaintance. What was she really thinking? What was behind her smile? Perhaps it was just put on. I study other wives and mothers. Some of them are at least mistresses of their own homes, if nowhere else.

I am a blank space even in my children's lives.

I walk in the garden and pick a basket of peaches. I look up at Devake's window. Hours to go, before he returns from school. I hand a few peaches over the fence to Veronica. She takes them with her lovely smile and rushes back into her house.

'I'm just getting tea ready,' she has time to say.

'We must have a chat in the morning sometime.'

'Yes, yes of course.'

I walk back in. I pick up the next book from the shelf. I have to finish it before the week is over. I love going to the library on Friday mornings. I love turning the pages of a book. I wonder who might have read it before me. Why did readers not leave a bit of themselves between pages? Underline a phrase that they'd heard before, or a paragraph that gripped them in some memory they thought forgotten?

'It's for me, Dad,' Devake says nervously. 'I'll pick it up from here.'

But Mahendra picks up the receiver from the family room and says hello. Simultaneously, Devake says hello.

'Hi, this is Nick. Dev at home?'

'It's me.' Devake's voice.

'He's not at home.' Mahendra's voice. Devake replaces the receiver.

Here's Mahendra now, at the bottom of the stairs.

'Devake, I have told you that this is study time. I have told you not to answer the telephone in the evenings. Why don't you listen? These good-for-nothings will hang on to you till you have some money to spend. And when you fail the exam, no one will be around. And then what are you going to do? Do you think they'll find you a job?'

I sit at my son's desk. I touch his papers, his books, skim through pages. The writing is often blurred by a net-work of black circles running in and out of each other, in places thickly coagulated, then merely outlined, sometimes shapeless, incomplete.

Lingering still, I pick up the scraps of paper lying around. Used film tickets, a crumpled serviette, a sketch of a bird, a woman's eyes, an unfinished letter. I piece them all together and make what I can of my son's secret life. I gaze out of the window at what he sees, as night after night, he sits here preparing for his exam.

I peer into a nightmare of fantasy and escape. Now he mumbles as in half-sleep, and plucks an image from some tune piercing his mind. His thoughts rush out, congest, turn incoherent and diffuse. I shut my eyes and ears. We all have our places in his journey through samsara. We pursue him, each in our own way, like hungry ghosts of a past birth, into dark, ever darkening, labyrinths.

His assignments are piling on. He dreads school tomorrow. What can stop Nick from telling all his friends about the dead-end telephone call? And then what else could Devake do, as Nelum would say, but put on his no-see, no-hear, no-care face that he assumes more and more often even with us? He sits in his class. He opens his books. But thoughts crash in, and sniggering voices. He listens to his friends laughing at his father. A real Hitler, he hears them say. He does not smile back or agree. For has he not been taught to be loyal to the family?

Often it gets too much to bear. Is it then that he loafs around Rundle Mall, crosses to Hindley Street, takes in a film, walks walks walks to Rundle Street to settle down in The Exeter?

Is this where he smoked his first cigarette? Ordered his first beer?

And gazed at girls. Yes, here they are. Chattering and laughing and tossing their wheaten hair, their moist red lips gleaming in the sunshine. He begins to bite his nails. Then, remembering his father's contempt, grips the sides of the table. Taps a staccato tune. Pulls out a pencil and a serviette.

I see daisies inside my head,
inside my head. Inside my head.
I've seen you once before.
You smile at me.
And when I look back, why d'ya look away?

He jerks back. He sips his drink. The froth lingers like milk around his lips. Glancing at his watch he folds and refolds the serviette in the shape of a small boat and sticks it in his pocket.

Getting drunk,
and I'm trying to stand up.
The sun shines on her when she walks.
Like a stolen picture from a magazine
I lost my dream.
Just like that, I lost my dream.
Here one minute, gone the next.

He must be home by four. To the timetable pinned on the board. To time slots filled in with maths tuition, chemistry tuition, physics tuition. To slots coloured in red: study, study, study. To someone's scrawl, 'Curfew', in the margin from six p.m. down: 'Don't call me, guys. I'm dead if you call.'

He finds no one home, but he hears voices, incessantly nagging. Cut your hair, Devake, close to the head and over the ears. Leave me alone, Mum. Pass the Matric, top of the lists, and into med school. Yes, Dad.

He turns on the CD. It invites him into a silver dream. Roll up, it whispers, and smoke up. He sings a snatch of lyrics as he sketches: the fear stops. The fear stops when a white eagle rushes out of the smoke and carries you somewhere you've never been. When you can't stand up 'cos of the fear, the white eagle swoops into your dark. You straddle its wings, and it flies into the light. With you. To the stars.

To the fucking stars …

He talks and talks. Breathe in, breathe out. He lets the music flow into his soul like the smoke he drags in. It pulses the veins; it flings the soul. On a high, swoon the lyrics, on a low. He changes to Nirvana. Distracted, he switches on the TV. Slots in a video. He gazes at the film clip. Fills himself with the hurt of a suicide. If he could do something like Kurt? Make the world listen. Think. Cry. And remember? Something, anything. The world lost me when Kurt gave up, he mumbles. On the screen, he sees this beautiful child in the long white cape. Kurt – confused and sad, the betrayed seven-year- old. Betrayed by the world. Lonely death-rocker, an image that tears at the heart. Kissing the muzzle of his gun. Another song, another singer. Hold a gun in your hand, and the world will be your friend. Sing on, sing on, your sad sweet songs. Life is a poppy.

The principal requests a special meeting with Mahendra and me. He is concerned that Devake's talents might be misdirected. Did we know that Devake was mourning so heavily for Kurt Cobain? He shows us the black band that Devake has been wearing on his arm. And holds open before us what I've already seen: an assignment that is almost illegible for the lines and circles eating in from the margins. The principal tells us we must try to direct Devake's attention away from this generation X, in which he seems to be getting more and more entangled.

What does he know? Devake explodes to Nelum. Fuck the world that nailed the hero and called it suicide. Kurt, I'll be at your altar.

He sits alone in the darkness. Mahendra switches on the light, one night, any night. Devake makes a nervous scramble to hide something. Too late. Mahendra pulls it out from under his shielding arms. I'm dead, Devake droops miserably. 'Please, Dad. Don't do that,' he pleads, he cries. My hours and hours of work and money. Photographs. Songs copied. Pictures pasted. Interviews. But Mahendra tears it all out of the album – page by beautiful page. I watch the shreds flung down on the carpet at our feet. 'Get back to your work.' Mahendra towers over Devake. 'How many months more for the exam? Eight. And what are you doing?' I bend down to pick up the scraps.

My son brushes past me, out of the room, out of the house. Breathes free. Walks the Adelaide night, the quiet winding roads. The roads sleep. Frangipanis cluster their secrets, like families. He wouldn't get lost, he whispers to me. I know, I know. I lean over him.

He is a little boy standing at the window. He sees a woman there, mist-shrouded, plucking frangipani for her Buddha. Swinging a branch here, touching a flower there. Pressing one to her lips. Mum's not Mum, he dreams. She's an angel flying to the stars . . . dying just to live. Can't see in the dark. Listen, I'm listening, but no one's making sense. He is Superman, he tells me, knocking Dad down, carrying Mum to safety. He tightens his arms around my waist. Oh, my son.

Voices in a nightmare. Give up, Dev, they mock him. Dev: try-hard, you wimp. He'll shave his head, he tells Nelum. What a dream. And he does it. Nelum laughs, hugging him to her, proud of him. Indulgent. Skinhead, she says.

I'm hurt and silent. Of course, he says, Sorry, Mum, for living. And Dad? See his face all clogged up? Now, that's worth seeing, he informs Nelum. Man, I feel good, he says, a human being at last. The school suspends him for three weeks. Mehandra rages: Devake, are you trying to disgrace the family? And I: Why, putha? Why did you do it? He withdraws into himself, totally. Tearing at his nails. Jerking his legs against the table legs.

I writhe now, in shame for my son, for myself, for Mahendra.

Wish I was Nel, he said to me once. No one pushes her around. She'll be married off to some Sri Lankan square. She's not going to need a career. She's okay. She's a girl. Lucky Nel, breezing through med school. Why must I beat her, huh? She's my sister.

He wakes up in the middle of the night to find me sitting at the edge of his bed. He gasps as if I was twisting a huge cord around his chest. I lay my palm on his cheek, and he sees my face in the half-light, ghostly and sad. His eyes grow all wet and soft. Mum ... Amma. Can't you sleep? I say no, I'm worried about you. His lips shape in a smile, a beautiful smile. I'm happy then, bending down to kiss him ...

Fatigued, I drag myself to his bed. I lie back against his pillows. I clench my fists tightly and in them, I crush my son's lament, his nightmares, his all.

D evake says nothing about the results of his mock exams. He has failed three of the five subjects. This, his prelude to the Matric.

Mahendra makes an appointment with his teachers. They look disturbed when he reminds them that Devake had to get perfect scores for most subjects. There are other courses besides medicine, they advise him. Perhaps Devake would be more suited to some other course? They talk enthusiastically about his love of music, and of his friendliness. What about a degree in music or the hospitality industry?

Mahendra comes home in a black mood. 'Do these Australians think migrants are only fit to cook or fiddle in their hotels?' he demands of me.

The exam is just around the corner. Devake's light burns on through the night. When he comes down in the mornings, he looks ghastly, with reddened eyes. His lips have grown thin and pale. His chest seems to have caved in.

The exam is here and now, at last. Mahendra is nervous and irritable. Devake glances uneasily at him. They get in the car together. Mahendra will drop him off at the examination centre. I walk around the car to Devake crouching in the passenger seat.

'You will be all right,' I murmur, my hand on his forehead. I whisper blessings. He moves impatiently away. There is a wildness in his eyes.

Devake has qualified for nothing. Nothing at all. He will have to sit the Matric again. He cringes and shrinks on the kavichiya in the lounge.

Mahendra reads the result sheet. Disbelievingly, he stares past me at our son. He moves towards him. He towers over him.

For no reason at all my wedding night is on me. When he raged and ravished my body. And ravaged my innocence with his contempt.

'What? What? What is the meaning of this? Is there a mistake? Explain to me. Explain to me. What has happened?' He pulls Devake up by his shoulders.

'I'll sit the exam again, Dad. I'll do better next year.'

Devake's voice is a mumble. His body is limp. Mahendra does not hear a word. His eyes are insane. He lifts his arm to strike.

'No, Mahendra, no.' My voice is terribly loud. He pushes me aside. I am thrown back against the wall. The front door bangs.

'It's you! You are responsible for this,' Mahendra turns

on me.

He is like a cobra. He strikes at my heart. I fall onto the kavichiya that Devake has just deserted. Its hardness hurts. Mahendra stands over me, flinging accusations.

'I am sorry,' I tell him. 'I am sorry.'

'What the hell are you sorry for now? You spoilt him from the beginning, and now here's the result.'

Left alone at last, I lay my head on my knees and twist my arms around it. I would escape into the montage of memory.

Sharpest of all is the fragment of my little son placing his toddling feet on mine and curling his arms around my legs as I sway to some music, back home. Clear and infectious, his gurgling laughter.

But I cannot succumb to the past. Not yet. I cannot let him loiter the streets in this mood. I would follow him, a ghostly presence withdrawn from sight.

Devake has no idea where he is going. He rushes up to the junction. Feverishly, he searches his wallet for his multi-trip. As he stands waiting for the bus, he looks to left and right anxiously, expecting his father to drive up any moment and order him into the car. Half hiding behind the bus stop, he tears at his nails. His head seems to spin. He feels nauseous and makes a frantic effort not to vomit. His body quivers and jerks and he clasps his trembling hands together.

An old lady approaches. She stares at him curiously until he moves out of the shadows. He sees her eyes run up and down his dress and he roughly pushes the loose end of his shirt into his trousers and pulls down his collar. Charmed by his effort, she greets him warmly: 'Beautiful day,' she says. He notices her pearly white teeth. Suddenly, he remembers the toothless smile of his grandmother, and her gentle touch. He returns the greeting. The old lady smiles back.

Devake ends up in Rundle Mall. He walks quickly over to its other end, searching the crowd as if he had arrived late for an appointment. He turns and rushes back.

He is just passing the two silver orbs decorating the mall when he feels someone's touch on his shoulder. He reels around as if stung, but his eyes register nothing. They seem in shock.

He does not recognise the man before him. He is about to vanish into the crowd when the man reminds him that they have met before. He invites Devake to sit with him on a vacant bench in the sunshine. Devake reluctantly agrees.

'Your parents and your sister okay? I have not seen them after I came to your house. You remember me? I'm Lal, Lal Gunasekera.'

'Ah, yes, yes . . . Yes, Lal . . . we are okay. I've got to go now. I'm late. I'm meeting someone. I am meeting someone.' He stares down at the road before him without moving.

He yearns for Lal to leave him alone. But obviously the man has no such idea and is going to cling to him. Devake remembers how his sister escaped these Sri Lankan acquaintances who buzzed around like gnats until they had extracted the family's most private secrets which they then passed on to everyone else.

And sure enough Lal asks: 'I forgot. You did the Matric. How the results? You do well?'

Devake collapses against the back of the bench. He leans his head over it, his thin neck stretching against it. He closes his eyes, and then begins to gnaw at his nails.

I feel it to the quick of my own fingers.

The voice persists: 'I am sorry I asked. You can do the exam again, no? It's all right. I also did my exam twice.' Devake opens his eyes: 'And what did your dad say to that?' he mutters automatically.

'My father told me, "Never mind, son. You worked hard. We'll try again."'

Devake hears the softness in Lal's tone and turns to look at him. His lips tremble in the effort to echo the smile offered to him.

'Is your father very angry? Don't worry, he'll forget about all that in a day or two.'

'Shit. Shit! Not Dad, man. Not Dad. We talking about the same guy here?'

In the silence that follows, Devake tries desperately to calm down. Already, he has said enough. His eyes dart here and there, looking for something, anything – for release from this man beside him, for release from himself, his father, his life.

The sunlight glints in the two big shining orbs. Buildings converge in them, and shoppers walk further and further into their depths. Like children in the Pied Piper story.

Devake feels Lal's arm move along the back of the bench. His stiffens his shoulders. The arm does not move away. Time passes.

A young boy leans against a post playing his flute. People drop a coin on the mat laid out before him. A wraithlike melody curls in the sunshine and evaporates. He is lost to all but the dream he breathes into his reed pipe.

Here, a girl and boy kiss intimately. In the shop window, elegant mannequins suggestively smile. A laughing child runs out of Hoyts, her hands full of popcorn.

Devake looks past her, and sees the mother following with the cap she'd dropped behind.

Gradually Devake rests back against Lal's arm. Lal begins to talk to Devake about his own life.

Mostly about his seven-year-old son who seemed to be adjusting well in his school. Did you have friends when you first came to Australia? Did you like it here? Do you go back often to Sri Lanka? he asks Devake.

Devake mumbles replies. He remembers bits of his past. How his mother had looked after him in those early years. His first day at school when he had flung his bag at the teacher and bruised her for trying to untangle his small hands from his mother's body. How he had looked for her as soon as the bell rang the end of school.

And how I never failed to be there when he raised his eyes.

A man selling balloons sidles up to him. Absently, Devake stares into the painted clown's face. A big red grin and two lines of black tears. As a small boy he would ask me why the clown cried and smiled at the same time. Even now, he found it pathetic, this confluence of smile and tears. Well, I would reply, life is about enduring. A smile, a tear, a sigh, the little boy's voice repeats, that's life.

He buys a balloon. It strains on its string. He lets it go. They smile, who see his gesture. In spite of himself he surrenders to the charm of the day and of the people. He tells Lal that he would like to return to Sri Lanka, but that it's too late now. He doesn't know the language, and what would he go back to anyway? All his friends are here. He looks around as if he can see them all, loitering here and there, waiting for him to join them.

And then, a few yards away from them, a young girl begins a dance. Sheathed in black silk, she tantalises the music to transform from pose to provocative pose. She is a blossom on a stem; a beast springing with ferocious grace; a glistening fluid gliding out of itself. At last, she stretches into something indistinguishable and ineffably beautiful.

Devake watches her fascinated. He yearns to merge with the girl's magically changing shapes.

Restlessly, he plucks his eyes from her.

Leave it. Subdue your desire, I would plead with him. Leave the seeing in the seeing, I would quote the scriptures. Let not craving enter into your perception.

But Lal's voice seems to merge with mine and quietly fade it away: 'See? You can be anything you want, here, in this country, putha.'

Devake springs to his feet nervously, and returns to the

red edges of his nails. 'I've gotta go now,' he stammers.

'Yes. Go back home now. Don't worry about results. You will do better next year.'

Devake takes the proffered hand. He shakes it limply, then watches Lal out of sight.

He sits back down again for a long time more. He leans forward on the edge of the bench, fists clenched against his temples. Beside him, the girl coils and uncoils to a quickened rhythm. People rest by his side, alone and in twos and threes. He hears them laugh and talk, and argue. Children make a great deal of noise, demanding things from indulgent parents.

If Nelum were here, she would snap the scenes into her memory and sketch them out later in the evening. She would ask him what colour that child's pinafore was, or nag him to remember whether there were clouds in the sky.

He blanks out his father's presence.

He turns round now, as if he feels me hovering in the shadows. And if I were there, how softly my hands would reach up to wipe the hurt from his brow, and how hurriedly he would turn and vanish into the crowd.

But it was his sleeping infant smile that drew me back to life, so long ago, and my mother's contented eyes as she placed him in my arms: 'A son, Manthri. How long we have waited for him.'

My son. I cocooned him against my breast and how richly my milk spilt over for him. Is it not said that a woman's life begins only when a son is born to her? Devake. We named him Devake, of and from the gods.

Numb with foreboding, I stand at the window, praying into the winding darkness, awaiting his return. Suddenly, there is light in the room. I no longer see the road but the windowpane, and, reflected in it, Nelum's face behind mine. Resentful of her intrusion, I pretend not to have seen her. A moment later, she switches out the light and goes away.

I look out into the darkness once again.

Mahendra sits in the family room. He will not go to bed. Nelum has called Devake's friends. She paces up and down. Up and down. No one has seen him.

In the early hours of the morning he returns and goes straight to his room. He locks the door. Mahendra switches off the lights downstairs, one after the other. Soon there is nothing but the darkness of empty spaces, and a sliver of light under Devake's door.

I walk over to Nelum's room. She is at the window, bending over and gazing out.

'Go and talk to him, Nelum,' I plead with her.

'No,' she turns round angrily. 'I won't do the dirty work now.'

I knock at Devake's door. I call to him, again and again. He opens the door. I step in. He closes the door behind me and turns unsteadily to his bed. I sit down beside him. His face is flushed and bloated.

'It does not matter. Nothing matters. Only that you are safe. Putha, Dad didn't mean it. Please, please,' I whisper to him. I would hold him close.

Tears course down his cheeks and into the pillow. I wipe them away. He turns his face into my palm. His shoulders shake convulsively. I draw my fingers through his hair. He does not say a word.

In the morning I find him lying unconscious in his bed. We rush him to hospital. I sit by his bed through the day. His lips are black with charcoal. He opens and shuts his eyes and recognises no one. He lies on his side with his knees drawn up, responding only to the nurse's clasp of his hand. He will not respond to mine. Last year in Melbourne, Nihal took an overdose of sleeping tablets after an argument with his parents. Like Devake, he had rushed out in the night. To this day, he has not recovered. I dare not turn my eyes away from Devake's face.

I carried you in my womb. I gave you birth and nurtured you, my son. Not for this betrayal, this denial.

It is days before we know about his future. He survives. He staggers out of the hospital leaning against Nelum; his face is haggard and stubbled. He is only eighteen years old.

He leaves the house in the morning; he returns in the evening.

He finds a job in a pizza bar. He hangs around with new friends who work part time like he does. Sometimes when Mahendra is not at home they visit him. I hear them upstairs, Devake's voice high above them all, laughing boisterously, luring them to song. He teaches them the baila that he's learnt on visits to Sri Lanka. He sings with an accent that makes me reluctantly smile. They turn up the music. They ask him for meanings. Often he invents something. The minute they leave, he grows deadly silent and gropes about his room.

He avoids the Sri Lankan community. He talks to no one in the house but Nelum, and not much to her. In the long nights he sings to the guitar, and I lie awake listening. As soon as he hears my tap on his door, he stops and puts out the light. I go back to bed and imagine him sitting by his window. The gaps, the vacancies, are also mine.

For Mahendra, he has ceased to exist.

Nelum hardly emerges from her room. She realises that her freedom must end with her degree. She knows that all Mahendra's energies are now concentrated on her. He wants to arrange a marriage for her. Before she gets out of control, he tells me. He regards me with contempt. Everything is my fault.

I follow Devake around in the house when he is in. He doesn't look well. I make him special dishes that he merely tastes. His lips seem to bleed like the ends of his fingers and the veins in his eyes. Occasionally, as he sits watching TV in the family room, I sit by him. He tolerates my presence.

I write to my mother to make a vow at the Dalada Maligawa. I will come down myself to fulfil it. My mother consults the astrologer. Through one of her friends visiting Adelaide, she sends me a suraya to tie round his neck. She has also sent us sweetmeats. The friend drops by with all these parcels and lingers on for a glimpse of Devake.

'Your mother told me that he is going through a very bad time,' she informs me. 'He failed his exam, no? So unusual. Generally, our children do so well abroad. Both my children somehow entered the university. What can you do without an education these days? It is so important that they do well in this foreign country, isn't it. I mean, isn't that why we live here? What went wrong?' She looks at me closely, as if she knew I was responsible.

She waits until Devake returns from wherever he has been and fixes her eyes on him as he crosses the room. He smiles slightly, with a tired charm. I introduce them. I feel shame and disappointment as I do so. I see my son as my visitor sees him. He is a failure, in her eyes and in mine.

I am a failure in everyone's eyes.

But my mother explains to me that the unpropitious time will pass in a year or so. I am consoled, somewhat. I tie the suraya round Devake's reluctant neck. After a few days, he removes it. He doesn't tell me where it is. Nelum says he probably sold it for the gold. The suraya is a sacred thing. Have my children no respect for anything at all? Not for religion, not for parents?

Mahendra walks about perpetually enraged. He has lost face with our friends. All their children have been selected for some tertiary course, if not for medicine, then for dentistry or law. They drop in curiously to ask us about Devake. They have not seen his name in any list in the newspapers.

With one or two exceptions, no one really cares. They

think that this is a good lesson for Mahendra and all other parents like him who expect impossibilities from their children. I yearn for someone who could understand.

I yearn for the temple.

I persuade Devake to return to school the following year. He would change his subjects, but Mahendra insists that he continue with science studies. What could one do with an Arts degree? He mocks. That is suitable only for drop-outs.

Nelum broods by the fire, one cold winter's night. She stretches out to the cassette deck, and restlessly seeks something to listen to. Loosened from its slot, a cassette drops down. She sees it is one of her father's old favourites. With a whimsical smile she plays it.

It carries her back to early days in Adelaide.

It is one of those splendid blue and green spring days. Small golden suns frolic in the stream. Devake is delighted with them and throws pebbles into the water, disturbing them and making them jump about. And Nelum? A little girl, skipping happily among the small sweet wildflowers in the grass. She laughs into her father's eyes as he kneels beside her. He smiles his rare, beautiful smile. Her laughter gushes out in reply and, like rainbow bubbles, blows around them. He lays a fin ger on her lips. She is all nervous anticipation. He switches on the cassette player. She stills to the music. She gazes around astonished.

The birds silently listen. The leaves pause in their floating.

He increases the volume until the song is a misty white

cascade floating down the sides of a precipice.

She turns back to him. His eyes are liquid. Together they listen to the vibrant voice.

'Listen, listen to the song, duwa,' he says to her in Sinhalese. 'He is singing about Sri Lanka. Listen, Nelum. He is singing of home.'

She does not understand fully the meaning of the song. But it is like sunlight, warming her with her father's smile. She will clap and dance. The music echoes away. He clutches her against him.

Now, she would run to him and talk to him about David, about David and her.

But Mahendra believes in duty and caste and religion. Race: he believes in race. Not in people nor in relationships. She has known that for a long time.

I withdraw into a deep depression. Silently, I walk away. We have relived one memory, and thought the same thoughts, but we have not exchanged a single word, my daughter and I. I lie down in the next room. I dream along the edges of impending nightmare.

Devake comes in with his guitar and settles down on

the sheepskin near Nelum.

'Where are Mum and Dad?' he asks her.

'Dad's gone to play bridge. Mum's lying down.' She lapses into her brooding. But he claims her again.

'I want to move out of home, Nel. What d'you think Mum will say?'

Nelum sits up at once, snapping out of her mood: 'What? Why? You can't. Where d'you want to go?' There had to be a reason.

'Oh, I don't know. Share a flat, maybe.'

His tone is nonchalant. Nelum sees how he hugs his guitar to him like his teddy.

'But why, malli, why?'

He is silent a long time. She holds out her palms to the hearth. It is freezing in spite of the fire. She is impatient for his words.

He begins to strum his guitar, looking at her, then looking down. She searches his face in the half-shadow. The firelight heightens the hollows in his neck and cheeks. She sees his eyes shine too brightly when they turn towards her.

She is again a little girl, holding Devake's hand. Was he anything more than two years old, back then in Sri Lanka? The wicket gate is low but still too high for them to look over. Its wooden bars cross diagonally, so they get a good view of the road when peeping through it.

Devake gazes at the road intently. Nothing much is happening. Nelum begins to lose interest. She looks down sideways at her brother, trying to think up a way to bully him. She could grab his teddy and run. He would never catch up with her. That would get him hysterical. But then she would have to deal with her mother. She didn't care, she could cope with that.

Devake's eyes are fixed on a small puppy in the middle of the road. Nelum is distracted. Where was the puppy's mother? It is a cute little thing – brown and white with little flapping ears. 'It's all alone,' she hears herself saying.

She wishes she could cuddle it. She is quite sure it is crying for its mother or brother. But they are forbidden to open the gate. She contains herself. She begins to relate to her brother a long-winded story about the neglected puppy. Clutching his teddy to him, he listens and she sees his eyes gradually begin to lose contact with the road outside. He often retreated like that, into his dreams.

Again they watch the puppy. It crawls about unsteadily on the road, then ambles towards the kerb. Soon it would disappear into the drain. They do not notice the lorry, until it is almost in front of the gate. They are only as tall as its tyres, if that. It looms before them suddenly, from nowhere, and the puppy vanishes from sight. Nelum feels Devake's hand creep into hers. Her fingers tighten round the small, moist hand. Then the truck has passed. But there is no puppy. Its body is flattened to the gravel. There is some blood. The lorry rumbles away. Red-brown dust rises and blurs the world, then settles.

She looks at Devake. His face is beginning to crumble. Nightmares are forming behind his eyes. He is going to scream in the night for the next two weeks. She has to do something. She is frightened by the way he looks. She tries to drag him away into the house, but he stands stubbornly as if rooted. She lets go of his hand and rushes inside.

'Amma, Amma,' she cries, 'come and look.'

Her mother comes running out of the house. Nelum bangs into her in her hurry to reach her. 'Where is malli?' her mother frowns. 'Why did you leave him alone by the gate?' Together they rush out. Devake has not moved. When he sees his mother he clings on to her dress and begins to sob. She puts her arms around him and lifts him towards her.

Nelum peeps through the gate again at where the puppy had crawled a few minutes ago. Disobediently, she opens the gate and rushes up to the dead little thing. Already, flies are settling on it. She gazes at its face. Everything else is smashed. She looks around again for its mother. She sees it far away, with its other pups. She turns back to report this to her mother, but there's no one by the gate.

Slowly, she walks back into the house alone. She hears her mother trying to comfort her brother. She goes into the play room and cradles her doll, Swarnamali, in her arms. Her tears fall on the little waxen face.

Now, Devake stirs Nelum from this memory. He pauses in his strumming. 'If I had my way,' he tells her, 'I'd be studying music at uni. Peter's going to specialise in vocals. God, I hate these subjects Dad's making me do again for the Matric. Or English, I'd go for English.' Assuming a languid pose, he recites for her: ' ". . . and when I shall die, / Take him and cut him out in little stars, / And he will make the face of heaven so fine / That all the world will be in love with night . . ."'

Nelum smiles a small sad smile, but interrupts him distractedly. 'It's too late, Devake. You can't change your subjects now, I don't think.'

'Sick of it, I am. Sick of work, sick of Mum, sick of Dad, sick of home. Man, to be left alone. Go on upstairs now, Devake. There's just eight years more for your Matric. Go on now, Devake. Six years more for Matric. Go on now, Devake. One year more for Matric. Go on now, Devake. Get into med school like Nelum!' Devake's voice cracks at odd moments. The last words are blurred, unintelligible. He struggles to steady his lips.

He turns from her and throws a root into the fire. It sputters little sparks and gradually subsides into the burning heart.

Outside, darkness falls swiftly. Devake draws the curtains. Shadows play bizarre games on the walls, like children in their sleep.

'I'm sorry,' she says at last. 'I just wasn't prepared, that's all.'

'Will you tell them then?' he asks her, laying his hand on her knee. 'Tell Mum first, and see what she says.'

Mum, tell Mum. What does he think Mum can do? Couldn't he see that only Dad said yes or no in this house, making them crawl up the nightmare of his ambitions?

Who knew that better than Devake? She sighs and touches his fingers. He turns his hand and cups it in hers. It is cold against her skin. The nails are bitten down, their ragged edges eating into the soft pale flesh.

'All right, I'll tell them tomorrow,' she says and sullenly returns to the fire.

He begins to pluck at the strings of his guitar: a note or two that suggest a half-remembered song. Vignettes of their childhood dance before her and she rubs her eyes to clear them. She gazes at him wistfully, protectively. His charm never failed with her.

The plaintive music glides into her like wine.

She lays her face against his shoulder, glad of his presence in her life.

For one moment more, my eyes cleave to them. I cut away the darkening edges, until all that is left is this sacred moment.

I thank all the devas that Devake has decided not to move out. I must write to my mother and ask her to organise a Bodhi puja so that further evil is warded off our house. It is a bad time for all of us. Devake is only nineteen. What does he know of life? I have protected him so much from the world.

'He's not old enough, Nelum, to live on his own.'

'And how is he ever going to be old enough if he lives here, Mum? You treat him like a two-year-old all the time.'

That is not true. Nelum does not understand. He needs me more than she does. He has always needed me more. And I know I must be there for him. This has to be her doing. I tell her so, and furiously she turns on me.

'I had nothing at all to do with it, Mum,' she lashes out at me. 'Go and ask him. Jesus!' and she stamps out of the room.

I am estranged from my daughter, but this is not the most important issue just now.

I compose myself. I go to Devake's room later that day. I must handle this before Mahendra hears of it. I am terrified of the violence that will erupt.

My son sits hunched at his desk. He does not turn round as I walk up to him. We look across at the garden together where Nelum sits sketching the splendidly blossoming wattle. I feel his hair. He is now letting it grow long. I dare not comment on it. He suffers my hand.

'Why are you trying to break my heart, putha?' I ask him. I can't keep the bitter excess of love from pouring out of my mouth. 'You are my only son, and now you want to leave us?'

Mahendra would say that this was the result of mixing with a culture that cared nothing for one's parents.

We should have returned home. Oh, we should have.

'Tell me you didn't mean it. Please, putha, don't do this and break my heart. You are not old enough to manage on your own. Remember what happened after the Matric results? No, no you can't go. I would kill myself for fear.'

And the loneliness.

I can't stop the tears coursing down my cheeks. Sobs thicken my voice.

His fingers clutch the edge of the table. He leans back against my breast. I hold him tightly.

In my heart, I know that my son and I are bound by something invincible. Nothing more is said about his moving out.

But, as I turn to leave the room, I see Nelum through the window, her face raised towards us. How long had she been observing us, her paintbrush clenched like a knife in her hand, her deadly yellow wattle incomplete? Even from this distance, I see on her face an expression that I will never understand or forget. If she hurled stones at us, or slung mud, she could not have hurt me more.

We speak mostly in Sinhalese, and she strains to understand. I would be silent, but Mahendra demands that I reply.

'But I think there is someone else, Mahendra.'

'Someone else? Someone else? Is she following in the footsteps of her mother, then? Is that what you have been doing, corrupting her?'

I imagine Nelum sitting up in astonishment. What were they on about? She would not hear my whispered reply, but she hears her father continue: 'The less said about that, the better. We both know what must have happened, but you'll deny it to your grave . . . How can you even consider the idea of Nelum having anything to do with an Australian? She's going to marry a Sinhalese. You know that. We've known that all along. So the sooner she gets all this nonsense out of her head, the better it is for all of us. Who's this fellow anyway?'

'He's in her year at the university. You have seen him once or twice when he dropped in to see her.'

'I don't remember, but this is what happens when you

open your doors to all and sundry. You should have advised her. That's your job. You let our son go to the devil, and now it's Nelum. You've just let things slide. Look at the Silvas. How well Ramani organised Sunithi's wedding. Ranil knew nothing about it till everything was settled between the two families. In this case, I've got to do it all, without any help from you.'

I sense Nelum's hostility: What is Mum doing? Did she sigh and turn away? Mum, say something. Do something. For once, stand up for me.

'Go and tell her now that we will arrange her marriage as soon as possible. I'll write to my mother and tell them to organise things,' Mahendra concludes the dialogue.

'You tell her, Mahendra. She will argue with me, but she'll listen to you.' I know my voice is strained and sad. 'I think that we should give her a little time, to get over this other thing.'

'Manthri, there's nothing to think over. If you give her more and more time, this thing with Peter or Harry or whoever lunatic it is will just go on. Don't you understand anything at all?'

'No,' I reply. It rings hollow.

Later, when they have all gone away for the day, I wander into Nelum's room. She is everywhere present, and unguarded in this, her private space. Occasionally, in the lassitude of my mornings, I relive her movements around us, her sudden involuntary gestures to connect with me, with her father, with Devake. And her withdrawal.

From her bed Nelum shuts her door with the tip of her foot. Her window is a leap into the sky. She leans over and opens it. Gumleaves slump on branches, brooding over everything.

She stretches her limbs and the touch of sheets on bare skin is the brush of wings. The butterfly dream. Her mother's voice floats and flutters about her and melts a story frozen in memory.

The child leans against her mother's knee and listens. Millions of butterflies fly to Sri Padha on pilgrimage and the world shimmers with their beauty for a heartbreaking moment. But they fly blindly and suddenly hit the mountain head on. They die in clusters of colour. Gentle and crooning is Amma's voice, fading far far away. Foolish butterflies, foolish butterflies.

The child tries to climb onto the mother's lap but her brother is already in it. She runs away hiding hurt-filled eyes. She returns less and less.

But now Nelum will try, one last time, to persuade her mother to change her father's mind. She walks into her parents' room and looks around. She hears her mother in the shower. She touches things – a pot of lavender; photographs of herself and Devake as children, imprisoned in ornate pewter frames.

Her parents' wedding photograph hangs from the side wall. She contemplates it. Marriages started off dressed up in pearly white sequins, and ended up stripped to bone.

The photograph is dusty. She wipes it with her palm.

Her father stands behind her mother in her white bridal glory. His hand rests on her shoulder. Nelum feels the hand bearing down more heavily on them each day.

She traces the heart shape of the face draped with white flowers and heavy gold head-dress. The eyes smile and do not smile. She senses their secrets. She would paint those eyes, she thinks suddenly, before he quenched them. She could cut him out of the picture, and make her mother sit alone.

She would then draw out layer on hidden layer. She stands by the mirror and looks at herself with the photograph alongside her. She sees her resemblance to her father. It seems to her that her mother had had no hand in creating her. And her eyes glisten. It would always be Devake, with her mother. That was nothing new. She had known this from the time she could understand anything at all.

'We all expected a boy,' she remembers her grandmother saying to no one in particular. 'Everyone was disappointed when Nelum was born. The firstborn should always be a boy . . .'

She turns away from the mirror. She sits down at the edge of the big bed, then picks up a newspaper cutting lying on the bedside table and reads it.

Govigama Buddhist parents permanently resident in Australia seek a doctor, engineer or lawyer, willing to reside overseas, for their only daughter, medical student, 5 ft 4 in. height, fair-complexioned, beautiful. Substantial dowry with a house in Australia. Please send horoscope and details of caste, religion etc. to . . .

Things had been set in motion, irrevocably.

Her mother walks into the room. Nelum holds out the piece of paper. Her mother takes it without meeting her eyes.

'There's nothing to be done, Nelum,' she says in Sinhalese. 'We are born with our destinies written on our palms.'

Nelum replies, as always, in English. Her voice crashes the stillness. 'I don't believe in that nonsense. Why are you doing this to me? Mum, you know I can't go through with this. Have you really put in this ad? Why didn't you ask me about it? I'm not a house that you can measure and advertise and auction off.'

'Dad wrote that advertisement, Nelum. I had nothing to do with it. We've received a lot of proposals. Do you want to see who they are from? Let's look at them together. We don't have to rush the wedding. You can have a long engagement.'

Infuriating, the pleading in her mother's voice.

'No,' insists Nelum. 'No, no, no.' She presses her palms to her ears. She looks about wildly. She would clutch at something, anything.

'What about David?' she asks after a silence. 'Mum. What about David?'

Her mother sighs. 'Tell him,' she says wearily. 'Tell him, child, and get it over with. It can never come to anything. Not with Dad.'

'But what about you, Mum? What about you? D'you also have nothing to say?'

'Nelum, talk to Dad if you want to. He will not listen to

me. No one listens to me,' she says.

Nelum looks at her sharply. Well, whose fault is that? she would demand. But suddenly she realises what her mother is saying. Wasn't she now in the same situation? Who was listening to her? Fleetingly, she feels her mother's hopelessness.

She turns to go out of the room.

'Do you love him?' her mother asks. 'Do you love this boy, duwa?'

Nelum turns around, startled. She hadn't expected the question from her mother.

'Yes,' she says.

'Does he want to marry you?'

'No.'

Nelum turns away with a sense of despair. Why does it have to be love and marriage? Marriage and children. But she wants to hide her face in her mother's lap and release her hurt.

She would tell her mother that yes, sometimes she wants marriage, but that most of the time she doesn't, not now anyway, not when she is so young.

'It can be perfect for us if only you could understand and compromise,' she would say. 'There are things I want to do with my life. Different from what you have done with yours. I want to specialise in surgery. I get Ds and HDs, even now in my sixth year, and that's not common. I want a career. But I can't specialise if I get married and have a child. Why don't you and Dad understand that? You brought us to Australia. We're not Sri Lankans any more.'

She moves reluctantly to kneel by her mother. She raises her eyes to the face so infinitely close but so definitely distanced from her. She senses her mother's withdrawal. She stands up. She leaves the room.

Why did I make no effort to detain Nelum? Or to persuade confidences? I watch her walk out of the room. I look down at my hands lying on my lap. Why did they not leap out to her? I, of all people, am responsible. For myself, for Nelum. I disturbed the clear still surface of my life long ago. Now I watch as the ripples fuse one into another, creating new ones, which spread and spread and spread. Inextricably interrelated. I let the moments pass.

Suddenly the room is strewn with flowers. I bend to pick them up. They are defiled, and smell of decay. I see my face among them and I crush them under my foot. A stale and vapid smell rises from them.

It is the same smell that rose from those sepalika flowers that had to be discarded at the Salgala hermitage when, on one of our visits to Sri Lanka, Mahendra, his mother and I were on pilgrimage. I remember ...

We watch the brown-robed monks climb up and into the forest after an almsgiving at the bottom of the hill. They speak no word, but look directly at the ground before them. Along the way, one pauses to pull out a creeper clawing its way up the steps. He twists it, stifling life, and throws it into the forest. At a break in the climb, another monk turns off onto a solitary side path.

Later, we too climb the stone path through dense forest. Occasionally, we detour towards a kuti. We spot the inhabitant monk from a distance. Slowly, he walks down the long straight path before him, his eyes cast down, his fingers on his string of beads. As the path merges with the forest, he turns and walks back. When he senses us, he walks into the kuti and closes the door, shutting out the world.

There is a flowering sepalika tree by the kuti, and a small shrine. The blossoms exude a strong sharp smell. In the clay lamp, the flame splutters. An alms bowl lies face down next to a chair. All is austere. I pause a moment by the small window of a cave walled up into a library. The monk must sit in that unyielding gloom, day after day, turning those pages yellowed with age and damp. I feel an inadequacy building up within me.

A dog squats nearby. They say that snakes slither around on moonless nights.

We turn back to the main path.

Mahendra walks in front, leading the way. He warns us now and then of a treacherous stone, a slippery patch. I help his mother with my hand at her elbow.

Low branches entangled by creepers crowd in on us, dripping heavy with the morning's rain. Small streams run down the sides of the path. I pause to dip bare feet in cool water.

'It is a long and difficult path, duwa,' my mother-in-law tells me. 'Look at the creepers, entangling everything like lustful cravings.'

I smile faintly and do not answer. Everything she says contains the message of the scriptures.

We climb on. Mesmerising, the gloom of the forest. Over the path hangs an unspeakably soft and ageless light that filters through the canopy of leaves. Whoever lives in this light, I think, lives sacredly. To leave it for wandering in the shadows would be to lose sight of nirvana.

'Sadu, sadu ... saaadu,' Mahendra's mother murmurs, overcome with awe. I am being transported into a realm of hushed tranquillity.

The radiant stillness is suddenly shattered by monkeys in the depths leaping from tree to tree in an oscillating dance of births and deaths. Then, with gleeful cries, they vanish from sight.

The light wanes and passes momentarily from the earth. A wild bird begins a piercing song. It impales my heart with its joy.

We lose sight of Mahendra. A sense of desertion, and of desolation, is upon me. I move closer to his mother, clutching the bag of flowers that he had picked so carefully this morning. It flattens against my body, offering no warmth. Uneasily, I try to hasten her.

'He's just gone a bit ahead. Do not be frightened, Manthri duwa. He will be waiting for us at the vihara,' Mahendra's mother assures me. She bends down and removes a leech clinging to my ankle. Swollen with blood, it lies senseless between her fingers. She places it on a leaf. Even a lowly leech has to fulfil its own karma.

And she pauses to rest. Gradually, she turns her distanced gaze on me. 'Every time you visit me, Mahendra seems to isolate himself more and more from everyone. Have you sensed it too? Is it something to do with your life in Australia? Isn't he happy in his job?'

My eyes jump to her face and crawl away. If only we could always blame someone else. But I know that she understands more than she ever reveals.

'Let us go, Ammé. There is still a long way left to climb.' I touch her elbow, but she does not move, and retreats into a past life.

'He was not always quiet, duwa. Such a high-spirited boy, always rushing in and out of the house.'

I have a blurred photograph of an adolescent boy that I removed from their family album and pasted in my own. He had moved impatiently as the shutter clicked, and projects a faint winged double.

'I had to curb him always. I did not want him to take after his father. I could never persuade Mahendra's father to go to temple, even on a maha poya, but I always took Mahendra with me, always. And every Sunday at the dhamma school, the chief monk himself indoctrinated him on the five-fold path.'

So, was the shadow obviated?

'Little by little, he settled down to be quiet and dutiful.'

Mahendra's mother leans against a rock on the side of the path. I stand at the edge looking towards the forest. May I escape into it from this upwardly twisting path and meander away, a mendicant in search of some other reality.

I look back, longing to return to the main road and sit in the friendly tea boutique, to taste a ripe plantain and hot plain tea. I'd throw the plantain skin to the monkey straining against the chains that bind him to his metal pipe. He is from the wilds but is almost tame now, the boutique keeper says.

We begin to climb again.

'That is why I was so anxious to marry him to a young Buddhist girl from the village who would be a good influence.' Mahendra's mother follows her thoughts. 'But . . . things are never what they seem, are they, Manthri? All is a maya.'

In all these years she had not exhumed the accursed truths of our marriage. At our homecoming she had not insulted me for denying her son my purity. She only clutched Mahendra's arm in horrified silence, as he explained to her that we brought back to her no stained sheet from our first night of marriage. They were an honourable family. They had never before been subjected to such humiliation. When she looked my way, what else could I do, but lower my eyes in shame?

Perhaps now, my refusal to share Mahendra with her makes her force my retaliation.

'The smell of mother's milk had not left his lips when he

married you – he was that innocent, Manthri. That is how I had brought up my son. But you . . .'

She speaks no more, but strips me of all that is private. She has the right; she is his mother. If she cursed me now, perhaps I may be expiated.

Emptily, I stand a step below her.

'We will have to atone for this crime against my son, each in our own way, Manthri. My sin is that I persuaded him into this marriage. But I did it in ignorance. I think I am paying already. I have only one son and I have lost him.'

We share that at least, Ammé, ignorance. And I have lost him too.

If only I could speak these words. If I fell at her feet and begged her forgiveness, would she help me up out of my guilt? So I could pick up the threads of life again?

But how can there be such easy solutions? Her last words, so swollen with unspoken accusations, hurl me into silence: 'It is too late, I think, Manthri, to make amends. I thought that by crossing the seas he would begin a new life. So I gave him my blessings. But how can we cross the chasm that estranges us from ourselves? And why am I speaking to you of these things now? It is just that I can't bear any more to see my son so disillusioned with life.'

Mutely, I succumb to her pain. Somewhere in the illusory wilderness, I glimpse a woman I've read of, whose despair led her away from all she knew to an unknown grave. She collapsed at its side and wept all day and all night, and so cleansed herself. By dawn, she had passed into another death.

Mahendra's mother sighs and wearily climbs, stone after inflexible stone to the summit. I help her on. She neither acknowledges nor rejects me.

The forest falls away, and above, very close now, we see Mahendra and the vihara.

We cannot use the sepalika flowers as offerings. I have crushed them and defiled them on the way. I empty the bag over the precipice into the forest below. My fingers exude an impure smell, and I wash it away at the well.

From this distance I watch Mahendra with his mother make obeisance at the statue of the Reclining Buddha. I know their chant, for is it not mine as well? I go to the Buddha as my refuge; I go to the dhamma as my refuge; I go to the Sangha as my refuge.

I have not the inclination to join them. And they do not look round for me.

We are only human, consumed by our passions, hatreds and delusions. It is only when we extricate ourselves from them that we may attain the peace of forgiving and being forgiven.

With a small pot filled with water, I walk to the Bodhi tree. Little by little I empty the water across my palm and over the roots. The last drops collect on the rim and trickle down.

In the far distance, on the pinnacle of the mountain, a bell begins to clang. It echoes from all around and beyond the surrounding forests. All else is silenced as though the whole world is paying homage at the feet of Lord Buddha. Mahendra's mother begins to chant aloud.

In the silence of my room, now, I hear the bells again, and the chant.

I awaken wearily as after a long night's journey. Let us leave the past behind. The present is upon me. And the future. In them, and in the bitterness collecting behind my daughter's eyes, I atone my sins.

Nelum's here, earlier than planned. She looks different; her eyes hold unfamiliar depths.

Mahendra was right. We should not have let her go for this holiday with her friends. Still, what choice had we?

'Nelum, you are not going anywhere with these "friends". Who has ever heard of a well-brought-up young girl from Sri Lanka going off into the jungle with a wild bunch of white kids?'

'I'm going, Dad. You can't stop me. I'm not a Sri Lankan and my friends are hardly wild.' She faced him resolutely and without fear.

'Is this how you have taught your daughter to respect her parents and her culture?' Mahendra demanded that I intervene.

'Do as Dad says, Nelum. Young girls don't stay away from home unprotected.'

She pushed past us. We heard the thud of her door.

Several of her friends have rented flats of their own. We had to hold on to what was left of her. We let her go for her holiday in the bush.

I watched her in silence as she left the house with her sleeping bag and backpack.

I watch her again, in silence, now she has returned. I follow her upstairs. Carelessly, she drops her backpack on the carpet and goes straight into the bathroom. I remove her grimy pants and shirts from it.

A few pebbles fall out. With them, the memory of her dream. I gather them in my palm, light blue and silver-veined, the sunlight caught within: pebbles more precious than jewels.

May I tread the fringes of her dream?

Nelum and David will not join the others this afternoon. They wander off alone. A creek at the edge of nowhere beckons. They balance along a tree trunk fallen across the river. Nelum is skittish and prances, untangling nerves. She feels on the brink of something. It is their second day out in the bush.

She offers him bits of herself at odd moments: 'There was such a domestic about this trip, David. I didn't think I'd make it till the last moment, y'know. Dad and Mum still don't know I'm here with you guys. I could never have come along if they knew. I only mentioned Julie and Cathy to them.'

'You're not in purdah, Nel. What've they got against men?'

'But that's how it is, back home.'

'Home?'

'Oh, you know, Mum's and Dad's – Sri Lanka.' She does not want to pursue the exchange and she moves uncomfortably under his quizzical words.

'You know, for someone who plays it kind of cool all the time, you're pretty mixed up.'

'No, I'm not.' She juts out her chin stubbornly.

'Okay,' he smiles, and looks away.

She is grateful to him for demanding nothing more from her, for not encroaching into her space.

Home, she must think, staring up through green into a spot of clear blue sky. Where is home?

'I'm going home, Mahendra. I can't live in this country any more,' Mum would say.

'This is your home, surely, Manthri. What are you talking about?' Dad would sneer.

'I'm leaving home, for a while, Mahendra,' Mum would say.

'Nelum, Devake, come and listen to this. Mum has now

two different homes. She's leaving home to go home,' Dad sneers.

Home.

'Now, children,' Aunty Pat at the Montessori says, 'take your colour pencils and draw a picture of your home.'

Nelum loves to draw. Aunty Pat gives her a blank white sheet of paper. She looks at it warmly. She fills it in with all kinds of colour. Yellow, that was her favourite. She takes the yellow. Then the red. Then the orange. And then, frowning, she takes up the black pencil.

Aunty Pat talks to her mother after school and lays the picture before her.

Nelum stands by with her thumb in her mouth. Her mother asks her to stop sucking her thumb. Guiltily, she removes it and puts her hands behind her back. She listens to them discussing her picture.

Her mother's face grows tense as she absorbs the image. Nelum wishes she had not drawn it. She would tear it up, but her mother folds it away in her handbag. Aunty Pat shows them what the other children have drawn. One, in particular, of four stick figures standing hand in hand in a flower garden in front of a bright pink house.

Nelum sucks her thumb all the way home. Her mother bends over her bed that night to kiss her lightly on the cheek. Nelum wraps her arms around her neck.

'Ammi, don't show the picture to any one,' she pleads.

'Yes, you must never draw another picture like that. See, everyone will think that there's something wrong with you, with all of us. You must never draw another picture like that again.'

Now, high up above her, the sky and the trees break up into fragments and merge into liquid patterns of colour. Nelum wipes her eyes to free them of the blur and turns to David.

She teases him, throwing bits of bark at him, taking all kinds of risks. He is sensitive and aware. They sit midway on the branch, their legs dangling down. He can just touch the water with the tips of his shoes. They hear the voices of the others fading into the distance. A somnolence spreads. The water is sluggish with fallen leaves and murky with shadows. All sounds are summarily suspended.

She droops heavily, conscious of his eyes and suddenly self-conscious.

She bends a branch to the creek and the water pauses, held and caressed by purplish-red leaves. She lets the branch swing back. The smell of ripe plums pervades.

She leans back on her arms.

The brush of shoulders and thighs.

The moist invitation of parted lips.

And blue eyes that dip into hers against the leafed gloom.

They return to the bank. They lie on the bare land that smells of sun and hay. She prefers it, that she is directly under the limitless blue sky.

It is almost evening.

He bends over her, blotting out the light. She would cleave to him, but he shakes free the constriction. Alarmed, she stares up into eyes as blue as the sky and as immeasurable. She returns to the body that is about to touch hers and rub against it with the harsh sun-burned earth under her.

'Close your eyes, Nel. Relax, you're all knotted up.' She closes her eyes in the sudden unknown and enters an intensely private world with him. Bold, roughly hewn: of endless skies and lands without black borders.

She closes her eyes on the moment. There is still the silence, the fading smell of sun on grass. They hold hands.

But, the distance irrevocably spreads. A dream lost on waking.

The cleared fields stretch yellow and dry before them. Far, far away, at the foot of the mountains, the bush secretes the unknown. Further up, the brown remnants of a bushfire show harsh against the green. Tomorrow, or the next day, she would hike into it with David. She returns reluctantly to the immediate.

He lies remote. She turns onto her side, her head cradled in one arm. She curves away from him and across the earth. She looks up beseeching – but remnant clouds drift in futile flight. And beneath, the land: ungiving. Her thoughts are inarticulate.

Despondence, a desolation.

And does she hear my voice, shocked, descending and blackly smothering her in a thick cloud? At home, marriages could be annulled for less.

She bites into her lip. She tries to smother the bile rising bitterly into her mouth. There was no reason for it.

She listens to Crooked River flowing sluggishly by.

Soon they hear the others coming back. Julie waves: 'Come on, you two. Time to eat.'

They scramble up. David lifts the end of his shirt and wipes the blood off her lip. For her, there is a curious intimacy about it.

He does not avoid or meet her eyes. 'Thank you for today. It was wonderful, Nel,' he says lightly, almost casually.

He thinks of it as a gift then. It strikes her that you do not expect returns when you give a gift. She tries to smile and complete their day as casually.

The others greet them with a shower of cushions and

lifted eyebrows.

They lie about the house after the long, endless day. Nelum sits by the window. The sky is a spray of stars.

In the distance the bush looms. She is at once repelled and attracted. A tree crashes to the ground. A disturbed kookaburra screeches, shocking the silence. The hush-flap of wings. The night sounds wail to the shadows once more.

'And what's your dad going to say about all this, Nel? He'll kill you. Are you going to tell him?'

She retorts playfully, but their voices, so light and full of laughter, so unaware of her brooding, plunge her into loneliness. David's part in the ribald exchange makes him one of them, different from her. Alone, she wanders a restless night. The bush seems to burst in from every window in the long hall dotted here and there with sleeping bodies. Resentfully, she yearns for the four walls of her bedroom.

The next morning, David tells Nelum that he wants to tour Europe over the next long vacation.

'Reckon we can do it together, Nel?'

'What? Tour Europe?'

Unbelievable! How did he expect her to work that one out? She imagines breaking the news to her parents. She blots it out hastily. But, sitting by David in this lonely spot, she imagines hitchhiking in Europe. Living together. Roughing it a bit. Doing what they wished when they wished. Two glorious months uninhibited by family. She thinks of Lucy and Rick. They seemed to be doing fine.

'Marriage?' Lucy would spit out distastefully whenever Nelum mentioned the word. 'Get a life, Nel!'

But now, she can't pitch into David's offer of Europe, and remains on its periphery. She gazes at him enviously. His face seems untouched by any kind of conflict and radiates a splendid spontaneity. For him all life is an adventure. She feels aged with the weight of her father's hand, her mother's eyes; and she withdraws into herself.

She leaves Crooked River that afternoon, looking back at her friends at the crossroads. She watches the four-wheel drive bump away with them and with David, and the cloud of red dust that swirls behind it. She had looked forward so much to this experience, and had struggled so hard to get to it. And here she was leaving it days early.

She sees the bus approach and climbs in. Outside, the landscape, so bleached by the sun, sears her eyes. A large black bird is perched on a dead tree. If her mother had seen it, she would have remembered how kingfishers perch like that in lonely places, back by the river in the village.

Mum is lucky, she thinks, leaning back and closing her eyes against the glare: she has Sri Lanka.

Nelum returns from the shower. I bring her a cup of coffee. She is careless with it, and impatient of my cloying.

'How was the holiday, duwa? Did you have a good time?'

'Yeah, it was cool.'

She sits at the dressing-table. She sees on it the pebbles that I have placed there. She touches them, then lets them be. I can't read her eyes.

She brushes her hair with short rough strokes. Impatient with herself, impatient with me. I move towards her but she shies back. Our eyes meet and part in the mirror.

It is the doorbell. It must be Devake. Relieved, I run down the stairs to greet him.

The nightmare reclaims, as always. The nightmare of amputated limbs and of phantoms that have taken their place. As time passes, the phantoms grow shorter and shorter and finally what remain are stumps with curled-out fingers or toes.

But the pain goes on as intensely as before.

It is pitch-black. I struggle up in bed to dreadful coldness. I feel for Mahendra. He lies away from me. I turn on my side. I must check on the children. Devake's room is locked, as usual. There is light in his room. What is he doing lying awake at this time of night? There's music seeping through the crack under the door, and the sweet smell of smoke. I tap at his door. He does not speak. He has locked himself in. Again.

Nelum's door is half open. She has forgotten to draw the curtains. The outside is a pack of shadow-hounds driven insane by the winds. The moon rocks to some wild rhythm behind trees. Leaves, like amputated limbs in a nightmare, rush about seeking refuge.

I close the curtains on the hostile night.

I turn back to Nelum. I touch her cheek. The skin seems to glow. Strange that I should think of Vesak lanterns gliding in the garden aglow with this inner light.

But her face in repose is like Mahendra's. So strongly moulded. If I were absent, perhaps Mahendra and Nelum would reconcile. Reconcile? There had never been a confrontation or an estrangement. I have always been the buffer. What if I left them alone now?

So strange a room. A room that Mahendra has refused to enter for several years. Was that when he lost control of Nelum? Had he ever controlled her? There was nothing here that you could pass over. A kaleidoscope of swirling bold sweeps. She tolerates nothing that is not of her choosing. The pictures on the walls, her dress, her books, her life.

'Mum, I think I'm having a period. Can I have a pad please?' The shock of the child growing up and requesting no protection. The shock of being excluded in her transition. There was no containing Nelum. No shielding her from evil eyes. No auspicious bath to cleanse impurities. Nelum with her cropped hair running off to school, embarrassed by the fuss. Nelum to whom becoming woman was nothing but the nuisance of a pad.

And for me? The auspicious bath time was at dawn.

Wrapped in a long white sheet, I am led out of my room

to the well in the courtyard. I am permitted to see nothing, but can hear the rustle of tender coconut leaves that the village women have woven in a curtain round the well. There is a hush, an anticipation. My fists clench excitedly.

At the well, the cloth is lowered from my eyes and wrapped around my body. The dhobi woman turns a pot full of flower-mixed water around my head. I am not prepared for the sudden splash of icy water or for the smashing of the pot. Startled, I stare at broken pottery, and limp flowers strewn around. I look worriedly at my mother, fear springing to my eyes. Perhaps it was an ill omen. But my mother smiles reassuringly: 'All the evil spirits have flown away now.'

Later, on the way back to my room, I split a coconut. 'Now, see that you split it in a single stroke,' the dhobi wom an advises. I bite my lip, lift the heavy long-handled kaththa and bring it down with all my strength on the coconut. The two halves fall apart showing wet kernel. The milk exudes drop by drop from the jak tree. The women smile. My mother touches my face with pride. I am a woman in her eyes. Bowing low, I greet her. She enfolds me in her arms.

But Nelum. I look round her room now. White walls. Pictures of people in unnatural poses: faces twisted in agony, embalmed in passivity. Lovers flying away on nude desirous wings. A twisted metal, shaped roughly into a woman bending over an infant. Lustrous windswept sunflowers. And high up on the curtain pelmet, the ebony Buddha statue that my father presented to her on a visit to Sri Lanka. I shift my eyes away from it. Why does she insist on keeping it in this profane room?

I am conscious of a further sliding. Can anything be reclaimed? Not Nelum. Without anyone's knowledge she has grown wings and how can they now be clipped?

I have nothing to do in this room any more.

The night wears on, surrendering to wandering unfriendly dreams. The walls converge in an unreal multidimensional way. Mahendra turns on his side and sleeps on.

The storm stills. The routine continues.

We sit together in the back yard with a biscuit and a cup of coffee, my cleaning woman and I.

'Had a good week, Manthri? Go anywhere? You never go out, do you, love? It's not right the way you live all cooped up inside.'

'Oh, I'm used to it, Marg. Where would I go anyway? I have my life all nicely cut out for me,' I reply with a smile that seems frozen. 'And what have you been doing?'

'Oh, I met this guy,' Marg says, wiping her lips roughly with her serviette. 'He's only twenty, and I'm pushing forty, y'know. Can you give me a bit of advice? I know I shouldn't be talking to you about my sex life over coffee like this, but d'you reckon it matters that he's so much younger and that? I mean, it mightn't show now, but what about when I'm, say, fifty?'

I give her my full attention. I jump headlong into conversation. How relieving to share a bit of life with someone, to exchange. To connect.

'Marg,' I hear myself telling her earnestly, 'it will not last. It can't. You can't just let yourself go like that. What about Shirley? She's older than this man you've met.' This is not what Marg wants to hear. She frowns.

'Who cares? Shirl moved out of home two years ago. Much she'd care. And anyway, I always say, it's my life, no one else's. I'll do what I like with it, thank you very much.'

I feel foolish. We talk a bit more. Nothing of consequence.

'Thank you for the coffee,' Marg tells me on leaving. 'Get yourself out of this house. You look in a bad way. Be sure and have a nice day, won't you?'

I pay her for the cleaning, and the extra half-hour of conversation.

Have a nice day.

The library is a wonderful place.

The supermarket is a wonderful place.

I have a nice day at the library.

I have a nice day at the supermarket.

I return to my house that is like a box. When I was very small, Thilakasiri caught a scorpion, and when I asked him not to burn it, he put it into a small box and closed the lid. When we looked inside again a few days later, the scorpion lay dead. It had suffocated because we hadn't pierced any holes in the box. It might have been kinder, Thilakasiri said to me, had we burned it before, in the usual way.

But I have seen that other fire-dance of the scorpion. They pour kerosene oil in a circle around it, and then set fire to the circle. The scorpion lies motionless in the centre. As the heat closes in, it begins to pirouette slowly in the circle of fire. Its shining ebony body turns a dull red in the blaze.

The circle closes in relentlessly, and soon the heat is unbearable. The scorpion writhes. It circles the inner edge of fire. Soon, it begins to spin, round and round, faster and faster. It stops in mid-motion abruptly, and leaps into the air. But there is no release.

Finally, it turns in on itself. In the last and fearful violation, it stings itself.

Another week goes by. Here's Marg again. She seems to be floating on air.

'Things are working out so well. I feel like a new woman. Darren's the nicest bloke,' she says.

I reply nothing.

Another week. Marg looks dreadful.

'What's the matter? Are you unwell?'

'God, Manthri, men! I tell you. Think they can take what they want and run off. It was just a fling he wanted. He's carrying on with a young girl now. But it's not the end of the world,' she tells me. 'I'll survive.'

And she does. She had the courage to sting herself.

Knee-deep in mud, he twists the stems and holds the blue lotuses out to me. My arms grow heavy with them. I hide my face in their fragrance, even now, even now. The burning sun, the water, the large green pads.

Dragonflies are little transparent kites flitting from leaf to leaf.

Dewdrops tremble at the edge of a bud. At the edge of petals. At the edge of my hair.

One bewitched night. My window looks out towards the moon-drenched river. I see them slide down into the soft wet earth that opens wide and receives them. In the grey light of dawn I bury my blood-stained phantasm where they lay.

One morning, I rush into the temple to lay my lotuses at the feet of the Buddha.

The chant. I can't recall the chant.

I tear out the lotus, petal by petal, and I see blood oozing from the delicate centres.

I sit with my mother on the long deep verandah. Dingiri-Aachi brings me a glass of coconut water, sweet and cool. My mother's hair is white. Her hands rest idly on her lap, the book of scriptures never far away. We listen to the temple bells.

'Come and live with us, in Adelaide,' I coax her. She smiles timelessly.

'This is my home, Manthri. All my memories of you are here,' she tells me. She sees a child sitting at her feet, and my father smoking a cigar in his armchair. She sees them like clouds passing by.

And, quietly, she removes her hand from my grip. Content – simply – to be. I do not envy her her release. It is rare and precious.

I wake up to Mahendra's arm lying heavy across my body. I feel like ash. There comes a stage when you just turn round. Stop moving forward. All that is to happen seems to have happened.

And you see a small mound of ash.

It is always a waste of time. We get in the car and drive home from the temple. We have nothing to say to each other. What will I do when Nelum and Devake finally leave us? How will we fill in the time? I lie down in bed, exhausted. I toy with the idea of returning to Sri Lanka for a while.

'I want to go home for a month or two, Mahendra. I have to fulfil a vow.'

'Vow? What vow?' Mahendra demands.

I hesitate to tell him. When I do, his laugh is mirthless and contemptuous.

'Other parents fulfil vows when their children achieve their goals. You fulfil yours when they fail.'

'I made mine for Devake to return to the family. Not for him to enter medical school.' I know my voice is empty even of bitterness.

He says no more. In his heart he is afraid to mock religion. Is he afraid, like I am, of the spreading hollowness? We avoid looking at each other.

'Must you go *now*, Mum, when bombs are exploding all over the country?' Nelum asks.

'There are still millions of people living there, Nelum.'

She cares then whether I live or die. Touched, I smile with her.

She rolls back her eyes as if I've done something foolish.

I leave for Sri Lanka. I will no longer have to walk the long narrow corridor with its closed doors. The first time Devake locked himself in, he was still a little boy. When he opened the door to step into the corridor, he fell over my legs stretched out across the carpet. I led him back to bed and slept by his side. He curled against me, secure. I drew my fingers through his hair and was content till morning.

I have begun to realise that it is not he but I who is dependent. With my love of him I built a husk around me. And lay secure in its warmth. But they skin the husk as it dries, layer by layer.

I have packed my clothes. I will be away for a while. I wait for Mahendra to take me to the airport. For some reason, I have asked them all to come to the airport. Nelum tells me that I am being melodramatic. But I made her promise to be there. I know that Devake also will be there.

Mahendra carries my suitcase to the car. I follow him with my hand baggage, heavy with presents for people back home and with presents for people I do not know. Why am

I trudging things for them? I am just too tired to refuse. It is easier to say yes to everything.

Nelum is at the airport. I smile and touch her cheek. She is taller than I, and thin. She has wispy hair, cropped like a boy's. She wears pants and a shirt all day and every day.

I suddenly see her beautiful. And vulnerable. Her face is set and lonely. She keeps a distance between us. That's so I can't touch her. Not even now, when I will not see her for such a long while.

'You are coming back, Mum. Jesus, why the fuss?' she will say.

We avoid contacting eyes. We both keep looking around for Devake. There is the final call for passengers. Mahendra walks up. He tells me that I had better get on the plane before it departs without me. He looks quite relaxed. Perhaps it is because Devake is not around. Or because I am going away.

'I will wait a bit more,' I tell him. 'Devake will come in any minute.'

Devake does not show up. I can't leave without seeing him. My voice rises hysterically: 'Can something have happened to him? An accident?'

'What accident? What nonsense! You know him.

Thinks of no one else but himself,' says Mahendra.

'That's not true, Dad. He'll be here. He said he got leave from the pizza place weeks ago. Why do you always accuse him of . . .'

The tension is tautly familiar.

A plane has just landed. People throng around the crowded doorway. Arrivals are such splendid occasions. I have missed seeing people so glad to see one another, so happy to embrace.

Someone pushes against me.

I have to get away. I gaze at the entrances. *Where is Devake?* I don't want to go away any more. I am filled with some fear, a premonition.

Mahendra picks up my bag and gives it to me.

'Go,' he tells me. 'You will miss the plane.' Nelum watches sullenly. I look around one last time.

'When he comes in tell him that . . .'

And he is here!

My son is suddenly before me. The bag falls from my hands and I clutch him to me.

He wraps nervous arms around my body, and bends to hide his face in my hair.

'Putha, putha. I was so afraid that something had happened . . .'

My emotion is out of place. As of someone going away for ever. But I can't move. Mahendra mutters angrily. Devake drops his arms. I pick up my bag and walk into the departure lounge without another word to anyone.

I look back.

They stand in a tight little bundle as if bound by thick rope.

Inside the plane, I locate my seat at last. Passengers walk up and down. A child with a teddy demands a window seat. Stewards smile artificially.

Things blur. I look out of my square of window and see a man signalling to the pilot. At this moment he controls my life: he will stop the plane; he will make it go. The plane begins to roll slowly. It is gathering speed. I cannot leave my son. As the plane rushes off the ground, I grip the seat.

I am lifted into the skies.

I bend over and into myself, gasping to breathe. I grapple with the seatbelt. It is strangling me. I must break free. I look about frantically. Everyone else is occupied: reading, studying the menus, gazing out of the windows.

I bite on my clenched palm to stop myself screaming.

Nelum told me years later that Devake had refused to leave the airport even hours after my departure.

He had sat on the carpet staring at the wall. Why did

they not tell me earlier? It would have given my life meaning.

Night falls in the plane suddenly, when stewards switch off the lights. Passengers turn anonymous; restless grey-blanketed slugs, wrapped up in themselves. No one needs anyone.

The sky is a vast dark space.

When he was a small boy, Devake imagined he was a star. I would cut out dozens of silver stars and he would paste them on black paper. Then he would point out to me a four-star family.

A family of stars shines silver out there in the blackness.

Home at last. To set foot on Lankan soil. Each time I come back, I know I have been away too long. It is a tranquil night. I walk the short distance to the terminal. The security is frightening. I have to avoid walking into a bayonet. They all seem pointed at me.

But here are my parents. I am back within the fold. The trolley is no longer my responsibility. Even I am no longer my responsibility.

My father has brought the Pajero for the journey. We speed along on Kandy Road. The roads are deserted. It is about two o'clock in the morning. Quietly, my mother tells me this and that about home. We correspond only occasionally across the seas. I hold her hand in the back seat. But my father is quiet – preoccupied. He is probably only half awake, at this time of morning.

The army hails us at a checkpoint. The driver pulls up alongside the kerb at once. My father looks thoroughly awake now. The army officer asks for my passport and stares boldly into my face. He scrutinises the photograph. His eyes return to me. They sear my eyes.

'Get down, get down,' he commands. My father is at my side at once. 'Get down, duwa.' His voice is taut.

'Open the back door,' says the officer and within seconds, four or five soldiers crowd around us. The driver's fingers are unsteady as he pulls back the door.

I turn the key in the padlock of my suitcase. My father bends over it and tries to unzip it. His fingers tremble so; I do it for him. We stand back as the officer digs into the case, around the edges. He holds up a bottle of perfume and a bag of chocolates. He leers back at me, hostile and mocking, as if I had no business to return home for a holiday. I have not the courage to confront his accusations. I look down at the road.

'Is it all right? Shall we go then? Thank you, thank you,'

my father says in a drained voice. He lays his hand on the officer's sleeve.

With something like contempt, the officer steps back. I am surprised at my father's words and actions. Time has passed since I saw him last. I remember him to be an arrogant man.

In a few minutes we are on our way.

'We escaped by the breadth of a thread,' my father mutters to the driver.

He turns round. 'It is a good thing you went away with the children. The Tigers are eating us alive.'

'We hear about the bomb blasts. Our area is still safe, isn't it?'

No one speaks. We wind our way into the night. It's a good thing we went away with the children, my father says. I try to imagine not having gone away.

We are home at last. The gate is padlocked. There are double locks on the front door and a ferocious dog in a kennel near the garage. My father makes doubly sure that the doors and windows are locked.

It is still good to be home.

The familiarity is excruciating.

This is the first time I have returned alone to the village after my marriage. People come around to welcome me. They talk constantly of relatives and friends dying in the war. Every family has sacrificed someone close. Then they remember to ask me about my life and family in Australia. Nothing I say seems to register. Everything I say sounds trivial and bland, even to me. So, they turn back to the war. And to fate.

I stand on distant boundaries peering in.

They see me changed. They gaze curiously at the shadows under my eyes. They wonder why I have come back alone, without the family. There is a growing sense of claustrophobia. I have faced my own war of betrayals, defeats, death of a kind. And I have become private. Once, I did not mind sharing my life with all and sundry.

I go down to the river, unheeding my mother's disapproval. I dip into the lazily flowing water. Here, at least, nothing has changed. The bath-cloth balloons around my body and I press it down. I loosen my hair and let it spread where it will. I open my hands upwards on the water's surface, languidly remembering. All, all that is familiar. The promise. The promise of life.

I look for the girl who grew up somewhere on these slopes. And for Thilakasiri, who carried her in his arms back to the house.

Those interminable days.

Stretched out like this my body trills like bird-song. I listen to the swish-swish of the banks sucking water.

It is dusk. The air is sultry and still. Tender na leaves are lips – soft and faintly red, vulnerable. I float in swelling waves of desire.

If only life could be an invitation, this luminous. If only.

It is my mother's birthday and mine. We go to worship at the Maligawa with plates of fresh flowers.

Nothing has changed, everything has changed. Soldiers swarm like flies. People go about their business, hurriedly, as if to meet a deadline. We are searched humiliatingly at the entrance. 'They are only doing their job,' my mother says.

A woman runs Thilakasiri's lotus stall. I buy some blue lotuses from her. She unfolds a bud for me with callused fingers. The golden heart of the flower is slowly revealed. She smiles with me as she sprinkles it with dew-fresh water. Tiny drops glint like diamonds in the sun.

I accept the flower from her in cupped hands. And my childhood.

I worship at the reclining Buddha. I arrange the flowers delicately in a remembered design. Flowers. Hundreds of flowers. In varying stages of freshness. I move away. I sit back on my heels. Bending forward, I touch the floor in obeisance. It is cold to my palms and forehead, and familiar. There is no effort. I lean against the wall with the other women. They smile and make room. Devotees mill around. Monks walk about in crushed yellow, gold and russet. On one visit to Sri Lanka, Nelum imagined that they were autumn leaves.

A sigh escapes the depths of my being.

A young boy walks in to offer flowers. He must be about twenty years old and looks like Devake. My eyes follow him. He smiles with me on his way out.

I am terrified that I can't let go.

In the deep nights when he has splintered the silence with his nightmares, I have hushed him. Then have I sat by his bed all night long, or lain beside him with my fingers weaving in and out of his hair.

I listen now, for his voice. It sings to me from his world. Sitting by the open window, he strums his guitar and sings into the hot summer night. His song is mine: a dream that brushes the eyelids with what was, what is, what must be.

I heard
a guitar
twanging in the distance
and I heard him strum
a tune
of
childhood dreams.
I felt
my mother's fingers
move in my hair
and
tears, hot in my eyes.

Mahendra is distracted by Nelum's presence in the room. He watches her covertly over the newspapers. She walks about aimlessly, touching the books that line the walls. He waits impatiently for her to settle down to something. She stops at her mother's shelves. Randomly, she takes out a book on Buddhism. She replaces it and moves to the next shelf. George Keyt's paintings. She turns a few pages. He returns to his newspaper and tries to concentrate on it.

He realises that his evening is in shreds. Resignedly, he folds the papers together.

'Dad, why don't you like George Keyt?'

It is an irrelevant question. He considers for a moment whether he should brush it away and return to his newspaper, but he feels duty-bound to instruct her through the paintings. The way he had Manthri.

'Bring me the book,' he says.

She sits on the cushion by his side. He pulls his chair slightly away from her. Mahendra always needs space and feels cramped when people sit too close to him.

He turns to the painting of the three monks.

'See how Keyt changes the entire concept,' he says. 'The monks are detached from life. They should be listening to the sermon undisturbed. Compare it now with this copy of the original temple painting. See what Keyt does: he shows one of the monks distracted by the woman and child. He shouldn't be doing that. His job is to concentrate on the sermon.'

'But, Dad, the monk is human. Surely his involvement with life can't be chopped off just like that, because he wraps a robe around his body?'

Mahendra is irritated by her slang, but he addresses the more important issue of instructing her mind: 'Yes, he must strive towards it. That's his purpose in life. This picture conveys the wrong message. It justifies the monk's attraction to life. That's the western influence. Keyt is not reflecting our culture or religion here, he's corrupting it.'

Mahendra gives the book back to Nelum and dismisses her. He couldn't do more just now. As in a reflex action, he blames Manthri for burdening him with this type of interaction. Surely, it was her business to guide her daughter along the five-fold path?

He returns with relief to the news. But she goes on sitting by his side, turning the pages. He is embarrassed by some of the pictures that capture her attention.

'Surely you have better things to do than to study pornography?' he says to her.

It seems to him only yesterday that he had said the same words to her mother. Contempt rolls off his tongue.

Manthri would look stricken and put the book back on its shelf.

'I am not a child any more,' Nelum retorts, and continues to gaze nonchalantly into the book.

Mahendra is acutely aware of Nelum's resemblance to Manthri. She had grown up without his awareness of it and he realises now that he knows nothing about her.

'Nelum,' he says, surprising himself, 'be careful with that book. It was one of your mother's favourites.'

'I'll be careful,' she says, clutching the book to her. She stands up at last, to go to bed.

He sits in the silent room for a very long time, thinking of nothing very focused. He finds it unfamiliar territory: being unfocused. He will snap out of it before it sucks him in. But just now, he surrenders timidly to the unfamiliar.

He feels Manthri, smiling, not smiling. And, perhaps, a sense of loss.

Mahendra writes without any emotion whatever of his brief exchange with Nelum. He wants to get rid of all my George Keyt books and paintings, because he will not have his children exposed to pornography in his own house.

I hold his letter against the light in a stupid attempt to read between the lines. I see nothing and no one but inflexible authority behind the writing. I remember a childhood game. Thilakasiri would write on a piece of paper with lime juice and let it dry in the sun. I would then hold it lightly against a flame and read his secret message to me. Thilakasiri. He had receded in these long years into a deep cavity within me. Now, in the humid still afternoons, in this familiar adolescent scene, he slithers around me at will. I am defenceless against the memory of the unfulfilled promise.

Mahendra writes that all is well, and that he is putting forward marriage proposals to Nelum, who is gradually beginning to accept the idea. He is quite happy that I am away with my feeble protests. He tells me to prolong my holiday. Even Nelum has not asked me to come over, nor Devake.

I am glad to be away. Oh, I am glad! I have not the strength to face Nelum, to listen to her anger, and to Mahendra's, or to be blamed for whatever crisis is about to explode between them. I have nothing to say on the subject anyway, but to agree with Mahendra. Nelum must succumb to her destiny. What was the use of bashing one's head against a wall? There is only pain. The easier way is to accept the inevitable. Only then can one move on to the next step: detachment. I am still a long way from it.

There is an almsgiving here, a wedding ceremony there, a funeral. I attend these functions with my parents but it is difficult to take up where I left off. People weave me into their fantasies of the envied and the unknown.

I am at crossroads.

In the mornings, I often visit my mother's shrine room. I sit beside her. She smiles quietly and distantly, emptying her mind of the immediate.

Afternoon. I lie sleeplessly in my old room, on my old bed. The yellowed net is held back against the four posters with thick cloth ropes. I toy with the rope. Its roughness is a seduction. I feel it against my neck. I rub it back and forth, back and forth until a welt begins to sting the skin. I stand before the mirror. It is no longer the shining silver surface it had been. The years have spotted it brown. I stretch towards it. It reflects a reddened neck. Once I had sought my body in this mirror – golden-skinned, untouched, unpenetrated. 'Like ran thambili,' Thilakasiri would say to me. 'Baba, your skin is the colour of ran thambili.' I look towards the rafters.

I think of how I used to get Thilakasiri to do all my odd jobs. Perhaps he would tie the narrow lengths of cloths to the rafters and help me hang from them.

I draw back against the bed. Memories dance on the wall. The rope twists and twists my neck like menacing, unrelenting fingers. Lie passive, Mahendra's voice commands, closing in on me – lie passive. I stretch out in bed and close my eyes. He grasps my hair and my body stretches until I can't breathe. Soon it will be over. Soon, soon. Let me die. At last, I wipe my sweating face with my palm.

These are long still afternoons. My father and mother doze in their rooms. The servants have gone to bathe at the river. There is not a breath of wind. Not a leaf shakes on the branches. I stare out at white sunlight on green. Then I close my eyes.

There is the laughter of children just outside my window. I must call them back into the house. It is too hot outside – Dingiri-Aachi will never listen to me. She thinks she can still boss me around. She must be grinding raw mango into pickle for them. It is too hot. I must get out of this bed and go to the window. But I am paralysed. Will no one fan me awake? I tear at my clothes, but they cling to my body, pasted in sweat. Suddenly I sit up. Devake and Nelum are no longer children. In the claustrophobic darkened room I feel my body wearied to the bone. The laughter outside fades. Dingiri is dead, has been dead for years. The tears pour down my face and onto my breasts. I get out of bed with all my strength. I see my hair in the mirror, hanging long and limp. I tie it into a kondé at the back of my neck in the old traditional way.

It is here at last – the moment that I have longed for, that I have dreaded. Nelum has finally agreed to marry a high-caste, high-class science lecturer from Ratnapura. He was introduced to her in Adelaide where he was visiting relatives. Everyone is relieved. My mother goes to the temple with a special offering. Mahendra tells me to stay on, and see to wedding arrangements.

Soon after their marriage they will go to England where Nelum's husband will take his postgraduate studies, and then they will return to Australia. Their life for the next six or seven years has been planned inflexibly. Nelum's dowry will see them through her husband's postgraduate years. And what of her? She will have children, of course. So, she will give it all up – her career, her dreams of specialising in surgery, all of it – and settle down sensibly, as Mahendra says, to being a wife and mother. There is in his voice a gloating sense of achievement, when he briefs me over the telephone. He is even thinking of transporting my father's majestic elephant to Colombo for the occasion. I have seen this fiasco before – an elephant lumbering in the gardens of the Galle Face Hotel – showing off all the bride's wealth to the groom's party. Mahendra has decided to have the grandest wedding possible. We will put on a good show, he tells me. Everything is so familiar, like the palm of my hand.

I have to admit that he is right – there is no other way for her. I am even full of grudging admiration for the way he handled Nelum. I would have tangled myself into a knot, to achieve nothing at all.

And my daughter? I speak to her on the phone. I ask her about the trousseau. Would she prefer to bring it over from Australia? She will wear the osariya, of course? The husband's family, being Kandyans, would expect it, and the traditional heavy gold chains. She answers in monosyllables. I fear to ask her about David, and she never mentions him. What future was there in it anyway? He had never offered her marriage. In the long sleepless nights I imagine she has realised the futility of it. Perhaps she will accept her destiny. Perhaps she had liked her fiancé on his fleeting visit, and decided to take the risk – she who loved adventure. Perhaps travel lured her. When she was a child, she longed to be a kangaroo, leaving us behind in a grand and graceful leap.

But I dream differently. Nelum, Nelum, how can you

accept your life laid out like a dung-coloured mat by your father? It cannot be, it cannot be. But if Mahendra has decided it, it will be. It must. I try to detach myself from premonitions that crowd the nights.

And they are here. Mahendra, Nelum and Devake have come to Sri Lanka for Nelum's wedding.

The wind dies. The waves crash and are reborn. The sunset is a smouldering pyre.

Why are we here, in this transiently lighted beach, my daughter and I? What more is there to be said?

Nelum picks shells, and treads seaweed. Back in Adelaide she will lay her new shells in her basket, and throw the old ones away. She picks only what's different and of irregular variegated colour. Restlessly she walks, now here, now there. She turns back. She bends down. The wind touches her lightly.

Leave me alone, Mum, her squared shoulders inform me, I have nothing to say to you.

I know she is terrified of the wedding, crowding in on her.

'Look at this wedding invitation, Nelum. Isn't it beautiful?' I asked her.

'It's a funeral notice,' she replied.

We have finalised arrangements for the wedding reception at Galle Face Hotel in Colombo. The poruwa, the drummers and dancers; nothing spared. It will be a very grand show.

She escapes to the beach. I follow her.

I sit on sand, and watch her. When did she stop running into my arms?

Her voice flings me against the rocks: 'You are marrying me off to a stranger, Mum.'

'We are born with our destiny written on our palms, Manthri,' my mother has advised me. 'What is the point of rebelling against it?'

I look into my palm. Why is my life twisted into a network of lines? Could I have changed what I was born to?

The waves lap around Nelum's ankles, and impatiently, she kicks the froth. Like me, she looks towards the sunset. Does she see it as the end of things?

I would say to her: forget Dad, forget custom, live your life, Nelum, the way you would. Go, go. Go, create your own destiny. I couldn't, but you can, my daughter, because you are strong enough.

She looks over her shoulder and sees me sitting on the sand. She smiles with me a rare unforgettable smile. Like a bouquet of flowers against a black winter's coat. I have seen her smile this way for David.

I gather the moment in my arms, in enchanted silence.

The wind, the waves, the clouds are stilled. There is only her voice, my Nelum's voice, echoing Amma, Amma, and her baby breath against my face. I raise my fingers in a caress. They brush a dream, a memory.

The clamour of the sea reclaims, and Nelum, in the mist of a receding wave. I shiver with some premonition.

What has she heard in the rush of wind that made her look back at me? Did I speak? Has she sensed my thoughts?

'Let's go, duwa. It's getting dark.' But Nelum does not move. Clouds spiral like smoke reddened by the sun.

People pass one another without making contact. I imagine it is the sunset.

They pay their respects at the pyre and move into the shadows in silence. Nelum and I must do the same.

Subject to decay are all component things.

Is it shame that we all feel? Mahendra's anger overrides all else. It is frightening, yes, and tragic, to see. In his own way, he loved Nelum. With a curious, detached kind of pride. He often wished she was his son, and Devake his daughter. She was like a boy in her ambition, in her determination to achieve, he would say, watching her stride across the earth. She made the sacrifice worthwhile. She realised the ambition. Because of her, he could raise his head in an alien land. But, because she was his daughter, he decided to marry her off. And now, he spurns her. Bringing her up has been a waste of energy, he says harshly, like cutting twigs to fence the river.

My parents seem suddenly old and grey. My father paces the verandah in confusion. Often, he holds on to the low walls. I fear that he might stumble. My mother sits staring vacantly before her. Times have changed since our day, she mumbles finally, in resignation. Watching them, I am grateful to the fate that created me dutiful. I have brought them nothing but comfort. I am content with what I have been.

Devake will not speak even when spoken to. He turns

angrily on anyone who dares to question him about Nelum's whereabouts. I think that he honestly does not know. But Mahendra will not let him alone.

In all this we have not contacted the police. Because we know, deep down, that we led her to this. Nelum has finally taken life in her two hands. Daily I wait for her, to hear her voice, to know she is safe. But she does not return. Mahendra blames me, only me. In the nights I dream that I am Nelum, that I have escaped with her. But there is no release. Not yet.

It rains and rains. The monsoons have taken over the world. The garden is flooded. Water, like milky tea, swirls around the front doorsteps. I remember floating paper boats with Karuna when I was a child, dipping my toes in the cold water to push them out. Later I'd fold them for Devake. Why don't I have any recollection of doing this for Nelum? The sky is overcast with massive grey clouds.

In the night there is lightning. The thunder is terrifying. The rain is ceaseless. Although she had never trembled in the storm, my heart gropes with fear for my daughter.

I never fail to go down to the river every evening. Perhaps I will find Nelum there, one day, any day, wanting to return home. I may glimpse a little girl in a bright-yellow dress, sobbing just here, under this na tree, for a lost dog or cat or bird.

Instead I see Devake leaning against a branch drooping over water. He aims pebbles expertly over the water's surface and watches them skim, two three four times. He throws a last pebble and leans back, his eyes raised to the tangled green above. His face is indistinct in the evening's witching light. I tread on sodden dead leaves. He turns round with a frown, then, seeing me, stretches back against the branch.

'I am frightened for Nelum,' I tell him. 'Perhaps she is dead.'

I grip at his hand. It falls limply to his side. Yet as I stand by him I am comforted, somewhat. His silence is a whisper. She is not dead. She is too strong for defeat. She has escaped us in the only way she knows.

'When are we going back home?' Devake asks me.

'Dad must return to work in a few weeks. Will you go with him? I must stay here for a while.' In case Nelum returns. Nothing seems more important now. But I do not say this aloud.

I watch Devake twist a leaf into a whistle. He begins to blow into it and the high-pitched notes pluck at memory.

'How did you learn that?' I ask him, distracted for a moment. I have seen no such homely whistles in Australia.

'Dad taught me when we were kids, when we used to come down here for our holidays. Remember? I used to ride here on his shoulders because he was afraid a snake would get me. You remember.'

No, I had forgotten. Carelessly, Devake flicks the leaf to the ground. It unwraps slightly and, damaged-green and wilted, lies on its wet grave of leaves.

I move down to the water's edge. The mud collects round the soles of my slippers. In the old days Thilakasiri would squat before me, remove the slippers one by one and scrape off the mud with a narrow stick. Balancing on one foot with my hand on his shoulder, I would smile down unrepentantly and watch his frown reluctantly fade. Had anyone ever indulged Nelum in this way? I am saddened for my daughter who grew up amongst strangers in a foreign land.

Devake follows me and bends over my shoulder as I kneel down to collect a handful of water. I look up sideways at him. He smiles a gentle smile.

My father used to say that it was when the shy beam of the crescent moon kissed the lips of a newborn infant that the first smile was born. I feel my father's fingers on my wrist.

The last rays of sunset dip into my palms. The evening shimmers, and vanishes into the night.

I release the water back into the river. A wind rises, leaves rustle and low branches brush the silk of water, distorting reflections.

I am suddenly uneasy.

'Let us go back. Vana Mohini must be on the prowl tonight. See, it is a poya night. You are not safe, out alone on a night like this.'

On the way back I relate to him how, on full-moon nights, the phantom Mohini stands with her infant in lonely places luring young men to their death.

'Wish I'd known her,' Devake chuckles whimsically. Just out of habit, I spit three times on the earth so his words will have no mal-effect.

He looks back at the river. 'Sometimes, I think we shouldn't have left Sri Lanka,' he says, curving an arm around me.

'Stay with me then. You can look for a job here.'

Hope – the fluttering wing of a dying bird, or a pebble sinking in the water.

'No,' he says, drawing away.

'All this will be yours, one day,' I pursue.

'One day,' he says noncommittally.

Late in the night, I see him by the river. Sleeplessly, I stand at my window. The full moon is adrift on serrated-edged clouds and bathes the night in milk. The sky is laden with stars.

If we are thinking at all, Devake and I, it would be of a night like this, many years ago, in Adelaide, when we reached, all four of us, for a glimpse of Devake's dream.

'Dad?' Devake shuffles into the family room.

'Can I have some cash?'

'What?' Mahendra's voice rises. His face freezes as he surveys Devake from head to foot.

'I want to make a telescope. The stuff will cost about sixty dollars. Can I have it?'

'By the name of Lord Buddha, what kind of clothing is that? Have you joined a hippie colony?'

'I want to build a telescope.' I recognise the rebellious thrust of Devake's chin.

'I will need a magnifying glass two inches in diameter and two feet focal length. I've read the instructions in an astronomy book. Thought of making one. Seems easy. Uh . . . I also want two tubes. You know, about two and a half feet long and two inches diameter. One should slide into the other.'

'Astronomy?' Mahendra says unexpectedly. He shifts his gaze from the skull-and-crossbones medallion on Devake's bare chest, to his eyes. Their usual wistfulness is replaced by a curious burning intensity. 'That's an interesting subject. I didn't know you were interested in it.'

'Oh, it's part of physics,' Devake says nonchalantly. And then, reluctantly, he shows Mahendra a diagram that he has drawn. Mahendra peers at it. Devake kneels by his side and explains the lines and angles. Gradually Mahendra's attention wanders to Devake's bowed head, so close to his face.

I see that Mahendra desires to touch the curly hair, draw him close. He lifts his hand. But he is used to distance, and he merely brushes Devake's head.

Our son, not aware of any of this, rushes on feverishly, caught on the unexpected tide of Mahendra's interest, stammering now and then.

'See? Shouldn't be too difficult.' He looks at me for support.

Mahendra's relief is very visible. Yes, he'd get all the material himself. Later, he tells me that he would do anything to get Devake interested in subjects like physics. 'Anything that will get him into medicine.'

A few nights later, Devake rushes into our bedroom. He stands at the foot of the bed, vigorously waving his arms. Nelum is already at the door rubbing her eyes.

Devake all but pushes us out of the house. He's got his telescope all ready and nailed onto a table that he has dragged out of the family room.

And that night, one after another, we seek the limitless sky through his telescope.

A profusion of stars in the small circular space of the lens. I hold my breath. It is like nothing I have imagined. A fistful of diamonds. Brilliant points of light sparkling softly, so far away, spilt carelessly into the darkness by a pair of magic hands. From behind, Devake places his palms against my ears, and suddenly my world is silent, without motion. I am a part of his wondrously glittering infinite dream.

Soon it is Nelum's turn. 'Gee, malli, how cool is that!' she whispers. I remember thinking how her eyes retained the stars in their depths. If only I had shared the image with her. Would we have smiled together then, for each other?

'A really wonderful sight.' Mahendra's voice glows with warmth.

I lift myself up on my toes to reach my son's cheek. He is already taller than I. I ruffle his hair.

Nelum wraps her arms around me tightly as we step back into the house. Did I press her close against me then?

They tell me that my daughter is here to see me. I have been teaching the dhamma to some girls orphaned by the war. I look out of the window. I see a tall young woman. My students regard me curiously. They had not known that I had a daughter. I will be back soon, I tell them. I walk down the corridor.

I stand at the edge of the temple building, wary and reluctant to go out. I look round. There is no one behind me. Only the bo tree and a Buddha statue. I have sat in its shade, day after day. In the drop of a bo leaf, in the flame sputtering in a clay lamp, I have seen impermanence. In the horror-filled memories of my students, I have seen impermanence. But I have seen it most starkly in the actions of my daughter.

Now, I see her. I walk towards her, this strange young woman. She wears a long skirt, not the pants and the shirt that I could never get her out of. A smile rises to my lips. She does not recognise me. Her eyes slide away. They search for someone else. Perhaps it is my white sari. Or my hair cropped short for the first time in my life. Suddenly there is recognition.

'Mum?' she says uncertainly. 'Amma.'

She comes up. The distance between us narrows. Closes. She does not know how to greet me. I take her hands in mine. She stares at me helplessly.

'Why are you here, Mum? Why are you here?' Her unasked questions stretch between us, beginning a remembered distance.

We sit on the low wall surrounding the bo tree.

'Mum, how are you?' she asks. She keeps looking at my hair, unable to comprehend it. We let it be.

Her eyes say, Amma, I had to go away. I was all screwed up by the wedding. I had to escape.

I have waited long for you to come to me, Nelum. A full year. Only waiting for news of you. Without knowing whether you were alive or dead. I have died many deaths. And now, I am again reborn. Into a curious detachment. I seek the tranquil bo leaves that rustle above, a drop of burned oil that drips from a blackened clay lamp.

Nelum and I – we sit side by side without touching.

'And now?' I ask her. 'And now that you have escaped? Where are you now?'

She looks down tensely.

'David's in the car,' she tells me.

Impatient as always, she would get it over with at once.

'We've been living together,' she says, her voice sharp and defensive. 'We are in Sri Lanka on a holiday.' Living together, she says. I hear the challenge.

I am not married, Mum, her silence insists, and you can do nothing about it. The victory is all hers. There is the taste of ashes. Of having failed, again. She searches my face. I say nothing for a long long time. I do not ask to see David. And I sense her resentment.

'D'you have nothing to say then?' she asks me.

'No. You are an adult now. You must do as you think best, Nelum.'

But you might have written to me, duwa, just let me know you were alive. I say nothing. I don't want an argument. I find that I don't even want to ask her about the year past.

I have learnt detachment, of a kind.

Her gaze is full on me. I turn down my eyes. I can guess her thoughts: How is it that Mum does not even ask what happened to me in the last year? Does she know that I returned to Australia? Doesn't she want to know? All she remembers is how I ran away from my wedding, disgracing them all. My happiness is not important to her. She will not understand.

'How is Devake? Have you seen him?' I ask her at last. Deliberately, I have excluded him from our conversation for fear of her resentment.

'Yes, oh yes, he's . . . he's working at . . . at odd jobs, part time.'

'Yes,' I tell her, 'I know that . . . but what else?' Her tone is reserved, and her face turns cold. It tells me more than I want to know. She still holds me responsible. Free him, she demands of me. Let him go.

I bend down for something to do. I collect a bit of gold sand from the ground. It slips through wide gaps between my fingers and collects in small golden heaps at my feet. Sand to sand. Powdery gold in small impermanent shapes. I try to reshape it with my foot. A clumsy effort.

Nelum watches. She loved this place when she was a child. She and Devake would gather the olinda seeds at the edge of the garden while Mahendra and I worshipped at the shrine. Does she remember?

But her eyes are blank of memory. They are focused on the moment. I feel old and tired. There is a sudden chill. I want, once more, to forget the body that craves the touch, the caress, the desire. I will return to detachment. I look for escape. I am being sucked back, without my consent.

'I'm working at Flinders Medical. I want to specialise

in surgery, Mum.'

She sounds defensive. As if she thought that I would protest, that I would insist that she got married instead, and had children.

'And Dad,' she says. 'I went to see him before I came over. He didn't talk to me. Devake says he doesn't talk to anyone any more.'

So he has not forgiven her. It is his way. He has forgiven none of us. But, again, I say nothing.

'You must come home,' she says, at last.

Her voice is authoritarian. I lift my eyes to hers. She wills me to do as she bids. How strong you've grown, Nelum, and how confident.

I sit with my daughter on borrowed time. We forget about David. He is patient and waits for her.

Nelum looks mature but restless, as always. I think of things to tell her but cast them away; they seem too trivial, or conducive to argument.

I am afraid of anything at all that will sever this infinitely fragile mesh that is gathering around us.

'Duwa,' I tell her gently, 'I don't want to return to Australia. I have found peace here in this temple and in my mother's house. I am at home.'

The mesh collapses. A maya. It had never been. Life is

186

but a futile endeavour to grasp the intangible.

'And what about home?'

Nelum insists that I focus on life. I try to control my trembling fingers. They pluck at the edges of my sari.

'I don't think I'm needed there any more,' I whisper.

'Oh, don't be silly, Mum,' she replies.

Pain moves in spasmodic waves, like an embryo struggling for release.

Temple bells die. Caressing the leaves, an araliya flower reluctantly falls. Last morning it blossomed white in the sun. Tomorrow it will be swept away, discoloured and malodorous. She stands up. I touch her cheek. Her eyes glisten. I expect her to fall on her knees before me, in farewell.

But she is not even a Buddhist. She is nothing, if not herself.

Who am I, but everything else?

She kisses me unexpectedly. I do not move away. I do not enfold her in my arms. I have waited so long for her to reach me. Is there regret? No. No. Had I not sought refuge in detachment? Now, suddenly, this desire to cling.

I bid her goodbye: 'The blessings of the Triple Gem be with you.'

She shrugs my hand away. The gesture is familiar, like the searing bruise that always accompanies it.

But I must make peace. I must speak: 'I hope you will be happy with David, Nelum.'

'No. No. We're breaking up when we return to Australia. He wants to practise in the country. He's taken up a GP's post. My work is in Adelaide.'

Is this her final victory over me? She turns and walks quickly out of my sight.

That evening, spreading the mat in my mother's shrine room, I strive to meditate. I know I have lost the way. I must return to them. I have not attained any form of detachment. This last year has been a delusion only. I believed I had renounced people and life, and purged the passions. I have sought and found nothing but the external refuge of a temple.

I lie awake. I seek the future. In the blur, the wheel turns and turns. I strain in vain for release, impaled on spokes of ignorance and craving.

I will step out of the plane, once more, and walk past sign boards. Customs. Arrivals and Departures. I have been in one or the other so many times before.

The plane has landed earlier than scheduled. I push the trolley past the crowd of people awaiting arrivals. They look sleepy but expectant. Desiring. I have seen too many welcomes and farewells. Here's another young family. Obviously an anxious husband and two children looking a bit lost as they wait for the wife and mother to complete the circle. Had my family ever looked out for me in this way? They had always seemed so annoyed, as if they had been hauled out of bed before their sleep had ended.

Mahendra is not to be seen. Perhaps he is still asleep. I will buy a cup of coffee. I sit down by the window with it. Its steam warms me just a little. I wipe the mist off the windowpane. The outside is still half asleep. The fog is clearing. Suddenly I can't breathe. I have come back.

I thread through the crowd gathering for another lot of arrivals. I have to step out. I can't breathe. My travel bags seem to have a life of their own. The trolley is so difficult to manipulate. There have been times when I did this all by myself with the two children hanging onto my arms. And I always managed. Now, it seems such a problem. I have to sit for a bit. Perhaps I should not have come back.

I face Australia once more. Like the first time, in the whitening dawn. But alone. The breeze fondles my neck, and stiffens it. I pull the collar of my overcoat tightly across my body. My knees seem encased in ice. I seem to be losing control of my legs. I cling to my trolley.

Mahendra.

My first question is about Devake. Mahendra tells me that he is visiting friends in Melbourne. Emptiness spreads into all the hollows of my being. When will he return? Mahendra does not answer. He carries the bags to the car.

We drive away. Linearly, the road stretches ahead. Symmetrically, the houses line the road. Systematically, the synthetic landscape soothes the eye. Underneath, the deserts lie, enslaved by an embrace unsought.

Mahendra carries the bags to the house. He asks me whether I will have breakfast. No, I tell him. It is too early. The silence of our marriage has solidified in my absence into something like ice. I have not the energy to force it to melt. Nor does he. I watch him as he moves back and forth from the car to the house. He does not glance at me even in passing. He dislikes my short hair, of course. He could never come to terms with Nelum's. His face looks haggard. His clothes seem two sizes too large for him. A lifetime.

I move to the mirror that has always hung in our foyer. Its brass frame is faded. No one has polished it since I left. Did they not know that it needed that bit of care? I don't suppose anyone ever saw me polishing it. I always did it during the day, after they had left for office or school or university. It's a job I always detested for the smell it left on my fingers, for the effort it required. I need not have taken the trouble. Yet it is with a vague sadness that I trace the dust on the frame. And the neglect.

I lift untidy wisps of hair from my face and stare into the mirror. I look different, of course. Imperceptibly, people grow old in body and mind. I have grown old without . . .

I must go upstairs. Mahendra has retired to bed. It is Saturday morning. He always sleeps in on a Saturday morning. Everything is familiar. Almost as if I have lived this life before. Am I reborn into a previous existence? But the wheel rotates in one direction only, so I am moving forward. I am at some intensely inward moment in existence.

I have got into the habit of sitting in the cafeteria close to the library before returning home. It is just by the main road and I sit in the window, every Friday afternoon. People drop in for a croissant or a slice of cake and coffee.

The woman comes in first. She is elegantly dressed and perhaps not so young. Her hair is black-brown and shines with an auburn tint. She sits at a vacant table and lights a cigarette. She draws on it as if wanting to let nothing of it escape her tasting. Her eyes are intense on the road. The imprint of her lips on the cigarette is like a bloodstain. Her dress is of some silken material that clings. She blows smoke from rich full lips.

The man walks up to her about half an hour later.

'I'm sorry,' I hear him say. 'I couldn't get away.'

'What did you tell her this time?' She lights up another cigarette. Her voice is beautiful: husky. But tense. Like her body. But it curls towards his. Like the smoke she blows out of her lips.

He does not speak. He only looks at her with angry hurtful burning eyes. It must be a familiar question and answer.

She says nothing more.

He orders coffee for them both without consulting her. They know all about one another. He suddenly cups her hand in his. She turns into it and their hands are lovers: seeking, withdrawing, embracing. Tracing patterns on skin, moist caressing secrets. Lying back with lips that part, open in welcome. And later. And later.

Like wading in a lake of purple-blue lotuses, water stirring against thighs.

Like lying by a river bank, wave after pulsing wave soaking the inundated body pressed against soaked inundated earth.

The man stands up and comes over to me. He straightens my cup, wipes the coffee off the table and bends over me. I see I have spilt the coffee.

'It happens all the time,' he says.

Reassuringly, he smiles at me. Unsteadily, I rise to my feet. I cannot meet his eyes. I do not thank him. I want to. I look back at the door. In the blur, I see him returning to the woman.

I visit the cafe again and again. They never come in. Perhaps they move from hotel to hotel, from cafe to cafe, to avoid being recognised.

In the nights I dream them. I see them etched against an

open window. I see her carelessly throw flowers to a woman begging for alms on the footpath below. And her intimate smile. I return the smile, and smell the sultry flowers.

The darkness is naked desire. I enter the margins of darkness. In the centre, entrapped in a web of flame, the scorpion dances as if possessed. I reach fearfully towards the centre. Her black-gold body twists and turns in agony, in ecstasy. The flames close in. Suddenly, all is empty, in an ever-spreading, ever-darkening emptiness.

And the man says: 'It is very difficult. She controls my life. It is difficult to come to you so often.'

I rise from my bed. I seek among my dresses a nightgown, long forgotten. It sheathes the body in a layer of lucent silk. I descend the stairs to the kitchen. I turn around. She blocks my way. She controls his life; she controls mine. Phantom woman: she rises from the ash. We confront, at last. We sob, we laugh, recognising past lives. I pierce into her. Her scream or mine slits the silence in a spurt of blood. Mahendra rushes in. I will escape his merciless grasping hands. I clutch at nothing. No one. Nowhere.

'My god, have you gone mad? Nelum, Nelum, come here!'

My life is an endless waiting. Waiting on them at breakfast. Waiting for them to come home in the evenings. Most evenings there's just Mahendra and myself. When did he let things slide? Devake comes and goes as he pleases. He is adult now. He smokes in the house and no one asks him not to. What does he do with his time? He leaves the house studiously, every morning. So beautiful, it breaks my heart to see him. Where does he go? He never answers my questions. He does not seem happy that I am back.

Is the cord broken, then?

But there are moments when he looks at me. Fleeting moments that make life worthwhile.

Nelum. Nelum is sometimes in, sometimes out. She asks nothing from us.

She attends to me clinically with long cool fingers.

'Your wounds have healed nicely, Mum. But look at the scars . . . Just be a bit careful about stretching or lifting things.' She gives me a tiny pill to ease the pain, and a glass of water.

Sometimes I refuse to swallow it. I refuse to look at her. I pretend she is not there. I seek the gums outside the window. Secretly, I watch her eyes beginning to worry.

'Mum's not too good this morning, Devake. Do you want to sit with her for a bit?'

Occasionally he does as she asks. But today he says no, he has an appointment. My heart sinks. Now I only want to be alone.

'Who with?' Nelum queries.

'That's my business,' he retorts rudely. In a minute the front door bangs.

I hear her on the telephone, telling someone that she will be late for work. 'Oh, an hour or two,' she says.

'It's nothing to worry about. Mum's fussing a bit.' She laughs: 'Yeah, just needing a bit of attention. Y'know, mind wandering again.'

She moves around the family room, looking for something to do. Annoyed that she is held back, like this, by a querulous, mindless patient. She keeps glancing at her wristwatch. It seems to have stopped. She shakes it and holds it to her ear.

I think of things to say, questions to ask. Then, I just stare before me, wanting her to go away to treat patients who need her more.

I raise my head. I really thought I had heard voices. Mine and someone else's. My eyelids droop. They get so heavy. I must remember that I am on these sleeping pills. They don't really put me to sleep in the nights, but they make me drowsy in the mornings. I can do nothing but doze in the family room. Nothing but doze and chat to someone sitting on the chair opposite. Sometimes it is my mother or my father. Sometimes it is that woman, brown-haired with red tints in it. Or Devake.

Thilakasiri. He never speaks. He is the dream. A dream that melts like an ice sculpture swilled in sunlight.

I must remember who I am and where I am. What am I doing here? In this house? Whose house? Who am I? Unsteady in the darkness at the edge of this emptiness? The ripples ever-widening.

Who is this running towards me, flying towards me, this bird of paradise? I would cage you, my splendid daughter.

'Mum,' she cries, 'Mum.' I stand up to greet her. She is vibrant. I am unsteady on my feet.

'I've got a school, Mum. I'm going to England. Oh,

Mum, Mum. I'm going to specialise in surgery in the UK. Can you believe that? Oh, Mum!'

I have never seen her like this. Nelum, in this sparkling mood. Nelum, so excited that she does not see my face changing, my heart sinking with her words.

'Sit down, duwa. Tell me about it. What do you mean, a scholarship? When did you apply for one?'

But she is not interested in details. Impatiently she tells me what I don't want to hear.

'I go in November, Mum. Imagine that. In November.'

And what do I do? I do not ask her why she did not tell me about it. I do not dare to ask her why she did not get permission. She does not need our permission any more.

How wonderful to control one's destiny in this way. How has her life been differently patterned from mine? Is this her karma just as mine was? Do I believe in karma any more?

I kiss her. I put my arms around her. Surprised, she bends to hide her face in my hair. And then, as suddenly, she draws away and into herself. She will not fall into the trap of my tenderness, pride, sadness . . .

She wings away to call her friends. I follow her flight, up the stairs and into her room.

My daughter: the surgeon. She has created her world.

All by herself.

'May the blessings of the Triple Gem shower on you, my daughter.'

But she's gone. Out of sight. She needs no one's blessings.

The house falls silent again. I can hear my own breathing.

I fall back into my chair. I open and close my fingers, to grasp her tiny fist in mine.

Mahendra. He says nothing now. He seems to have lost the will to protest. I don't know whether I am relieved or just tired. His passivity and his defeat are his own. He has lost his power over me. He tells me that he might be made redundant in his office. He might have to retire. That would give him just that much more time in the house. I find that I don't care about it one way or another.

I only care about going to the library. It sends me into a depression if I miss out on my Friday morning at the library. I browse among the shelves. The books are mostly old friends now. I talk to them, and they tell me that I am one of them.

Not my old Buddhist texts. They gather dust on the

shelves. When I have the time I will tear them apart page by page. I don't have the energy just now.

I think about Mahendra and his retirement. It would make him richer than ever. Even now, we have more money than we need. A lot of it lies in the bank, unused. There is nothing to buy, nothing to spend it on. Perhaps he stocks it to ensure a future for me in a nursing home.

Here are the young missionaries at the door. Ah, yes, I had forgotten. They visit me once every few weeks and try to convert me to Christianity. I listen to them. I ask them no questions. They give me Bibles and prayer books. They remind me about my soul and all that Jesus has sacrificed for it. They tell me that the church is a welcoming place for lonely souls. Occasionally of a morning, when it is open, I wander into the church. I sit on the hard wooden pew and look around at lonely praying lips. I know their prayers. I pray that they will be heard. Sometimes I take with me a candle. I light it at the foot of the statue of Mary. She grasps the body of her dead son in her arms. I have never seen a face so sad. My candle makes a small glow in the chill vast church. In the end, I scrape out what's left of it. A small heap of wax in my palm.

Only my son has hold of me. He can lead me where he wills. Sometimes he helps me to bed. Sometimes to the shower. I will not allow Mahendra to touch me. I will not let him lay his hands on me. Because, what will he do next but torture and torment? Stab until I want to die, nothing but die?

Disconnected from all. Wandering spirit seeking some other husk in some other existence. That's what I am.

And my son.

I wipe his face when he sleeps and my fingers erase the lines of pain at the edges of lips, at the edges of eyes. The edges of reason.

Together, we wander the hills in the nights. We pause by a streetlight sometimes, and in its light we seek lost tracks. We wander endlessly, in a never-ending samsara. We hardly speak, for words have lost all meaning. He is tired.

We sit down among the willows. He stretches back. The night is cold and clear. A crescent moon seeks release from the clinging arms of the dying full moon. Occasionally a waterfowl skims across the water, churning silver-black ripples. The willows silently droop. There is the distant murmur of people walking up or down the road, connecting with one another. I take Devake's hand. His fingers involuntarily clench mine. A smile, a sigh. He lays his head on my lap, and sleeps his tired sleep away.

Dawn spreads iridescently across the sky.

Have we got used to the idea that Nelum will never return permanently to Australia? She writes to us from England that she is coming down for some conference. She will use the opportunity to visit us. At the airport, after her last visit, she said to me: 'Dad just sits, Mum. He doesn't talk to anyone any more.' She thinks it's time he stopped brooding over the past. She would have us all function normally, so she can be comfortable with her life. But I judge her harshly. Who would not want to be part of a functional family?

Leaning forward, Mahendra draws back the curtains and the autumn morning floods into the room.

Automatically, he notes Manthri's absence on the bed by his side. If she were there, she would immediately open her eyes and gaze out. He has covertly watched her sleepy eyes as they filled with the sunlight, and how she would raise her arms to run her fingers through her hair. But that was when her hair was so long it flowed down to her hips when she sat up.

He does not linger in bed. He has to get ready for Nelum's visit. She has to visit each one separately, he thinks cynically, for do they not all have lives of their own now?

After breakfast, he steps out of his house. From the gate, he looks back, almost from habit, for the face behind the window. He sighs, and shifts around for something that might interest him, and hold his attention. But the road is as it has always been, with the wattle by the hedge. Soon it would burst into yellow puff and buzz with bees. When Devake lived at home, he would start sneezing as the first pollen spilt out.

He walks further down the road towards the open fields. He sees a lost-looking kitten clinging to the edge of a garden. He recalls how Manthri carried back to his mother's house a baby squirrel that they had found deserted somewhere, and how she had sat up through the night crooning to it, feeding it milk from a rolled-up shred of cloth. He recollects what, in spite of himself, he had abruptly noted: that the eyes of the little squirrel held the lost ache of their son.

He shuffles forward. All the neighbourhood is out gardening this morning. Those who know him greet him cheerily. He does not stop to chat. He tells no one about his daughter's visit.

He pauses now and then, feeling frail and grey. He will

not admit to loneliness. He looks around again. There is a woman seated under the reddening tree. He watches absently, as she stretches out her hand for a leaf floating down. She holds it to her eyes, and through it, seeks the sky. Her lifted face, the slightly parted lips . . . He recognises that gesture, that inward involvement, that connection.

He turns the corner. He forgets the red light. A car swerves, and he halts, blinking, in the middle of the road. 'Lost it for a minute, mate? C'mon, let's get you across.' Jack rushes out of the deli. He frowns, but takes the strong arm.

Mahendra stands at the bakery. The window is dressed with cakes and bread. What would Nelum like? Perhaps that sugar bun? And if she had asked Devake to come along as well, what would he like? And Manthri?

For a moment, he forgets that she is back in hospital.

But then, she had never liked what he gave her, like the saris he presented to her when he returned from visits to Sri Lanka. Gradually, she would wear nothing else but the colours he liked to see on her. He remembers with a shudder the flamboyant shades that she preferred in the early years of their marriage.

And the desire she spurred and spurned.

The humiliation of the aftermath, of listening distantly to her subdued sobs, he remembers that also. How he distanced himself, but how, inadequately, he wandered aimlessly from death to death. Of the other, her adulterate treachery and her denial of it, he will not be reminded.

He has not forgiven himself, nor her.

He remembers the almsgiving on his father-in-law's death anniversary. As the monk chanted blessings, he and Manthri and her mother had clustered round the mat to tilt the water into the bowl below. As the water overflowed the sides of the bowl, he had seen Manthri's mother wipe her eyes. 'I am like a flower gone stale, Manthri, now that your father's light is extinguished,' he had heard her say. He wished Manthri had her mother in her.

He keeps standing at the shop window until he realises that the girls in the bakery have noticed him. He walks in embarrassed and buys the first thing he sees in the counter: a walnut loaf which he knows will probably lie untasted during the visit and go stale in a day or two.

Manthri would buy flowers for the evening. He stops at the florist's, protesting against his gesture. What would she buy? What would be appropriate? She would spend a long time deciding. He would wait impatiently for her outside. He would be struck by the shine in her eyes as she returned to him, her arms full of whatever flowers were in season.

'Those flowers will be dead in less than a week,' he

would say, extinguishing the brightness. 'Wouldn't it be better,' he would continue coldly, 'to donate that money towards some charity?'

Now his eyes sweep over the flagrant mess of colour around him. Giving in to an unfamiliar impulse, he buys more than is necessary, and then feeling foolish walks out quickly. He'd avoid the neighbours, he thinks sourly, by taking the longer route.

Evening. Early darkness. Any moment now, Nelum would ring the bell. He reminds himself that he is not looking forward to this visit. They reminded him only of the futility of life.

He turns on the heater, just warm enough for an autumn evening. He dresses methodically. He chooses brown trousers, a russet sweater.

He glances around at the spacious lounge. It looks garish tonight, he thinks distastefully, with the mass of scarlet blossoms in the corner. It almost feels like all the family still lives in it. He tidies up here and there – all things in place – the heavy brass vases that had lost their shine through the years, the photographs on the piano, newspapers and magazines on the rack, cushions neatly piled on the sofa.

No longer did the batiks adorn the walls, nor brass trays repose impressively against the mantelpiece.

Yet, in the deep gloom of one corner hangs the old oil painting that Manthri's father had commissioned for her. The Bible Rock, partly covered by ephemeral mists, rises against the pale intangible sky from the wide vista of hills. Terraced paddy fields stretch down the valleys. In the foreground blossoms a mara tree, and beneath it, three women walk down a narrow path with bundles of firewood balanced on their heads. As he contemplates the painting, it seems to Mahendra that the deep-red blossoms and the women were out of place in the stillness that permeated the landscape.

It had enchanted Manthri. She refused to believe that it was a commissioned work. He was certain that she imagined the artist actually standing by Kandy Road at dawn, armed with easel and brushes. She would inform visitors that the artist had known her as a child and had painted her into those endless fields.

'There,' she'd say, laughing at herself, 'do you see a small girl with long plaits flying like a kite over those paddy fields? That's me,' and absurdly point out some non-existent image. Interrupted briefly from a political theory that he had been expounding to someone, Mahendra would turn up his eyes at this trivia.

Now he draws close to the painting and searches in it for the nebulous image of the child hidden in the dawn-misted fields.

He dusts the painting. The artist's signature is scrawled in one corner. He had died many years ago. Mahendra wonders what would happen to this painting once he and Manthri were no more. He had not realised that it meant anything to him. Perhaps they could donate it to the art gallery in Sri Lanka where it would be at home and cared for.

Sri Lanka. Memory is a sigh that expands and expands within him, until it chokes him out of breath. The island's face bore no resemblance now, to what he remembered. In his absence, it had changed into something almost as unrecognisable as the friends and relatives he had left behind. Neither he nor Manthri has visited it for many years. With parents dead, there was nothing to go back to, after all. No one knew them any more. They were nothing more than a social obligation to people who had been their friends. The distance between was too vast to cross in a five- or six-week vacation. The last time, he had felt like a tourist, hiring cars and visiting interesting sites. Living out of suitcases – booking in at Sigiri Village and Habarana, Bentota Beach and the Oberoi – in and out of hotels.

He looks for some music. His Sri Lankan cassettes have mostly deteriorated and not been replaced. He puts on an Irish ballad that Nelum had presented to him on one of his birthdays. She had visited Dublin, he remembered. His children always gave him what they wished for themselves, he had later complained to Manthri.

'Yes, just giving you little bits of themselves,' he remembers Manthri's reply. She always had this way of twisting the truth into something incredibly disconnected with reality. Even now, he feels impatient.

He stares out of the windows at one of Devake's star-gazing nights, then draws the curtains.

She is late. He wishes she would come in and get it over with. Ask about his health, his heart condition. Had he changed his medication? When was his next appointment with the cardiologist?

Yet, he listens to the sound of her walking up the road. He hears her footsteps on the gravel path. She'd have to push back Manthri's late summer roses hanging over the path. Will she stop to smell their fragrance as her mother would? No, he knows that, impatient to reach the door, impatient to reach the bell, she'd let the petals scatter behind her.

The bell. Out of habit, he waits until it rings again. He stops in the middle of the room. He calls Manthri to escort him to the door as she always did. Then he remembers. Wearily he walks up to the door.

Nelum kisses him awkwardly on his cheek. He does

not respond. The first thing he notices is that she has grown her hair. It falls below her shoulders. He sees a rose petal caught in it and lifts his hand to brush it away. As a reflex action, she pulls back, tossing her hair. She sees her reflection in the mirror before her and removes the petal, dropping it carelessly on the cabinet.

Mahendra leads the way to the formal lounge. They sit opposite each other. He suffers her technical questions about his heart condition, and replies in a word or two. She asks to see the latest prescriptions. He refuses, and is satisfied when she is silenced at last and withdrawn.

'Nice flowers, Dad,' she smiles suddenly, moving towards them. 'Are they for Mum?'

He does not reply. When she smiles, unexpectedly like that, he feels Manthri's shadow touch her face.

He observes Nelum from under his brows, morosely, while she touches the flowers with her beautiful long fingers, her surgeon's fingers, and rearranges one or two stems. She steps back to survey the re-creation. Is there the glimmer of pride in his eyes? He knows that she has just addressed some conference. Occasionally, she sends over a paper-cutting with her photograph in it, or a journal that had published her research. He reads every word and contemplates the contents for days.

But he hates these achievements for which she had renounced his ambitions for her. He hates her for not being his son. He lowers his eyes.

After a while he seems to forget that she is in the house. She makes them coffee, and cuts the walnut loaf. Politely, she takes a bite or two from a small slice and leaves the rest on the saucer. She drinks her coffee, sitting before him like a visitor.

Devake does not show up, as usual. They do not talk about Devake. He does not tell her that he has emptied his mind of his son. He notices her glance often at her watch. He does the same, more often than she, wishing only that she would go away to her world, and relinquish him to his.

He hears a car in the driveway. He sits up very straight and listens.

'That must be Devake,' he tells Nelum. 'Will you open the door for him?'

'It's the taxi,' Nelum replies. Her eyes turn sad with a passing repentance. He droops on his chair, pitifully exposed, as he realises that she had ordered the taxi beforehand, that she had slotted him into this one hour.

'I'll be visiting Mum tomorrow,' she says on parting. He still stands at the open door, long after the taxi has driven away.

He turns, and sees the rose petal on the cabinet. He

looks at it for a while and then places it in the centre of his palm. Clumsily, he tries to smooth out its bruises. Its fragrance lingers faintly. And, mingled with it, the perfume that she wore.

They tell me that my daughter is coming to see me. They've got me ready to meet her. They sponged me down and dressed me in my best gown. They've brushed my hair. They held up my mirror to my face. When I took the mirror from them, they cluck-clucked indulgently and left me.

The mirror has an ornate frame. It has a history. I must remember to untangle that one day. Just now, it is simply a surface that reflects. My face has always been curiously heart-shaped. I look for her now, the woman with the heart-shaped face. I would like to see her again. How irritating that I can't find her. When I look in the mirror I always think that I am looking at someone else. I can't get used to this person who looks so different. We face each other. I am nothing like her, nothing at all. But sometimes I talk to her, and she listens. She smiles and cries. Sometimes I want to touch her. She seems so close, so familiar. She tries too, and our fingers look as if they meet. But they don't, and that's sad. It's all a mirror, you see. A game in the mirror. But today I must pin down my mind for my daughter's visit. Today, the mind must not be allowed to meander.

My body feels quite comfortable and happy. This is how it will look, one day, in a funeral parlour. All washed and ironed. They sponge it night and day. They keep it pulsing with injections and tubes and things. When the mind is absent, I lose the body, and have no need of it. But they do. It's the money, you see. My body feeds them and their families. My full-time nurse has four children, the part-time one has two. They tell me I am fortunate. I am in need of nothing. I crave nothing.

The clockwork life here deadens craving. Everything is routine, everything points to the hands of the clock. Sleep, wake up, bedpan, shower, dress, swallow pills, lie down, eat, wheelchair out in the courtyard. Sleep, wake up, bedpan, shower, dress. . . And now, in a few minutes, a visitor!

What more than to have my only daughter visit me for an hour or two each time she passes through, about every two years. Pull yourself together, she will tell me if I start crying. Pull yourself together. Don't be so weak, Amma. Or will she call me Mum? Don't be weak, Mum. Amma, Mum. Amma and Mum. So different these two. Worlds apart. I have been both. Or have tried to be both. Strong as Mum, weak as Amma? Don't be weak, Mum. How do I know that she will say this to me? Mahendra would say it too. But not my son. Not my son. What would he say? Hide his tears in my hair? Wipe mine away? My son. Beloved, my son. He will see the heart-shaped face in the mirror. He will be able to touch her. I must write to him. I'll just jot it down, in case I forget.

Darling putha,
(Fill in the page.)
Yours, Amma. Always Amma.

Here she is now! She looks like a sprig of spring flowers. She seems to have grown taller than ever, my Nelum. And dressed in a sari. A sari! She always refused to wear it. I never gave up trying. She hated it. I am filled with gratitude. I know she is wearing it for me. Tears spring easily to my eyes. She leans over me, touches her cheek to mine, coolly, elegantly. She has let her hair grow. At last, at last. It is a soft caress on my face. My tears spill over. Her perfume lingers. I breathe it in in in, into a bottomless, endless craving. I will breathe it out when she is gone and surround myself with it; the perfume, the smile, the sari. The child sucking her thumb. The embryo curled in my womb.

She sits down on the chair by the bed. Not *on* the bed. Hold my hand, Nelum. Here we are now, running in a shower of leaves. Autumn leaves, dipped in scarlet and gold. Here's one that falls with a touch and a smile. And your laughter, lighting with silver the edges of grey cloud. And back home, the bo leaves, my eternal friends, pressed between the leaves of my book of scriptures. And my father saying to me, 'Look, duwa. See how the leaf fades from green to brown? That's how transient is life.' How transient. I stopped calling Nelum duwa a long time ago. I have a name, Mum. Call me by my name, she would insist. Later, all grown up, she still hated it when I occasionally slipped. You take away my identity, she would tell me, all grown up and self-confident. I am not duwa. I am myself: Nelum, Nelum, Nelum. How like steel, her newfound self. It had always been so gentle for me, back home. Come, my father would smile, come and pluck these flowers with me, duwa. It is time to go to the temple.

But Nelum's here. She leans back. She removes her handbag from her shoulder. This is what she must do every morning in her office. She must take her bag off her shoulder like this, very professionally, and set it on the table. And then, draw on her long white coat that must hang behind her door. And someone, perhaps a nurse or secretary, comes in to be ordered crisply by her, my daughter, the surgeon.

'Are they feeding you well?' she asks me. Nelum, dear

Nelum. Why should they not feed me well? Have you come halfway across the world to ask me whether I am well fed? Do I look half starved?

Yes, I tell her, they look after me very well. A routine question, a routine answer. Doctor and patient.

'What a beautiful sari, Nelum. Where did you get it?'

'Oh, this old thing. It's one I got in London, I think, or was it Tokyo? I don't remember, Mum. I've had it for ever so long. I wear it now and then, when the weather is right.'

My daughter travels a lot. Research, conference papers, publications. They are beginning to know her around the world.

But I remember now, about the sari. I got it for her myself, on one of my trips back home. I remember even the salesman who held it against my body, and how I draped it before the long mirror, speculating about it for Nelum. Lost in the distance of time. Something that I will seek in the endless summer evenings, when the spiders spin their webs all silvery gold in the sunset, outside the window. When it is hot and still. Not now, not now. She looks so lovely in the diaphanous sari, a gossamer thing. And . . . what's the word? Elegant. She had always wanted to be elegant.

'That's so elegant, Amma,' she would say, touching my sari when she was little and thought me perfect.

She glances at her watch. So secretly; it hardly hurts. She looks around the room and sees there are flowers.

'Who sends you flowers, Mum?' she asks.

Her lips curve in a smile that I had thought forgotten.

'I do,' I tell my daughter suddenly, surprising myself. 'I do.'

Every Mother's Day, I send myself flowers just so I don't forget that I have been a mother, that I have given birth to a son and a daughter. And on Valentine's Day I send myself flowers again so I don't forget that I have been married. Just so I don't forget the transient in the permanent. That flash of colour. That intense moment. That enchantment. That transience.

'You send yourself flowers?' my daughter asks. Her face works a bit. Is it put on? Was it practised in her third-year medical course? I regret telling her the truth about the flowers. I should have kept it to myself. Perhaps she will tell all her elegant friends about it, that her mum, the poor soul, sends herself flowers.

'Mum looked a bit off-colour, this time,' she'll tell them. 'Think I'll order her a bouquet of flowers every two or three weeks.'

She leans across the table for the Yellow Pages. Florist, florist. Ah yes, David Jones. Why not? Let us be elegant.

'Tie it with different shades of ribbon each time,' she tells the florist. She remembers that I love colour.

'Yes, charge it to my account, of course. Thank you.'

'Well,' she turns back to her friends, her lover, her who-ever of the moment, 'that's taken care of.'

And yes, I will love them when they arrive in a rush of colour. 'Each flower . . .' I will tell my nurse. 'She chooses each flower for me, every time, with her own dear hands and sends them to me.' I show off the lace-edged card: 'With love from Nelum.'

She smiles kindly, not taken in. And in the coffee lounge, she tells her colleagues that the poor thing in room 36 is slipping again. 'She's quite fond of me,' she will say. 'Gives me some of the flowers to take back home. They're from her daughter, y'know. They say she's a surgeon some-where.'

Their voices whisper down the corridor to me. I have all this time to think about these conversations. Dialogues, snatches of songs that happen around. Don't whinge, my daughter would tell me if she knew about all this. That's what gets me in a state. This having to keep it all to my-self. Sometimes, I call a priest. They keep waltzing around with their vacant faces just waiting to get all pink and con-cerned. They love to touch hands, press mine into theirs.

But where's the comfort in that? They've been trained to do it. But they listen. And they look kind. And I bring out my best smile for them.

'Dear Father,' I recite to Father Frank, Francis or Patrick, 'such a pleasure to talk to you. You make me feel so tranquil.'

They go off well pleased, my smile pinned on to their collar. Dear lamb, they must remember over their spartan meal late in the evening. She just needs a sympathetic ear. Lives like she has no one in the family but a weed of a son who bludges off her. She's not in her dotage either. Mind keeps going, that's all. Very strange, very strange. Must get into knots of loneliness.

True. Terrible painful knots, Nelum, that refuse to untangle. I do try. I have this great tangled ball of wool of various colours. I love to try to untangle them.

They bring us tea. This is a special occasion. Tea in the room, in lovely china cups. Things seem to blend beautifully; the roses in the vases, the roses on the cups. My daughter confers with the nurse. It is all very professional. The nurse speaks to her deferentially. My daughter moves to the foot of my bed, reads the chart, rustles a paper.

She will speak to my doctor before she goes. Just to check. It's like watching the TV, black and white sharply etched close-ups of people's faces. I've seen it all before, many many times.

'I hate it here, Nelum,' I tell her, after the nurse has gone away. But she has heard all this before. The urgency in my voice, the clutching. She leans over me, as usual.

'Amma,' she says patiently, 'do you want to come with me to London, then?'

Another routine question. Again, I breathe in her perfume.

'No,' I give her my standard reply. 'Not unless Devake goes too.'

She sits back. 'Of course,' her lips curl cynically.

'You will visit him before you go away?'

I seek her hand but she avoids contact. Even that is very routine.

'Yes,' she says sullenly. 'I'll visit him, if he's home.' She looks out of the window at the brooding gumleaves for something to do. I touch her face with my eyes and trace its features. She has a heart-shaped face! I see this suddenly. I lean for my tissues. She turns back to help me.

Yes, I know, Nelum. Let's not talk about it. Your brother is weak and helpless, unlike you. And you detest him. He wanders in sometimes and asks to see me. The nurses here are kind. They often let him in, even if it is past visiting hours. He sits on my bed, nervous and weak. He cries and talks to me. He needs money, and I give it to him. He goes away. His eyes are glazed almost all the time now, and he smells strange and sweet.

Nelum's eyes grow stormy. You don't understand. You blame me for everything. For what he has become. For his failure. Like your father did. Just like your father did. Your eyes grow resigned. Yes, let it be. Let us leave your brother alone. Leave him to me, and to this life that he will not leave behind. Not for you. Not for me.

In a minute she'll be gone. Dearest Nelum. My child, my daughter. So young and confident, so cool and elegant. Unlike me, all knotted and tangled. But I've found the heart-shaped face that was lost somewhere in the mirror, in the wool, and for which I searched. And here you are now, right before me. But you would hate that. You want to be yourself, as always. That would start up an argument, and I am tired of arguments. We've had enough. No, just go your way, my lovely blossom. Across oceans, ride the crests of waves. Leave me. There's the spider now, busy outside, spinning. It's going to be another long summer evening.

Nelum stands up. She picks up her bag. She is going away again.

I must let her go: 'Visit malli, duwa, before you go.'

'Bye, Mum,' she says, turning at the door.

I search for the heart-shaped face. It's gone. They give me the pills and the tangled wool. My hands are cold and cannot grasp. The nurse begins to massage them. She begins to croon to me. My eyes move to the window and seek to settle somewhere beyond the cobweb, beyond the gum.

I listen to myself crying in my sleep. I don't know where I am. I see a vision of my mother's face. And who is this man who beckons to me from the old lost track? I crawl up but a woman is twisted like a vine around him. A scream rises deep within me, and I run away. Is this Mahendra standing by the bed? His face is a mask. It is like death. Will this be the result of what I was? What I am? Am I? Am I not? In what birth? What existence? What death? The walls loom closer. I shred my clothes. Who is that laughing? What are these wheels, spinning and spinning? Will they never stop?

There is only a song, coursing through my blood – a serpent piercing, coiling into my body. It is my song. I meander in the night. Wild woman with streaming hair, naked and languorously stretched in the moon-light. Spreading circle beyond circle . . . into the void.

The house sleeps. But I sense movement. They say restless spirits visit by night and reluctantly take leave with dawn. I am the silence of those who never sleep.

I have been lying on my side for so long, my body aches. I would close my eyes but they cling heavy-lidded to the wattle outside. An ashen light envelops the garden and the wattle is a golden haze, as if it were wrapped in veils. In what different shade and mood have I seen it in Nelum's paintings. What dreams have been mine as I gazed into it all this time. Now, at last, the veils float away, one after another, and the wattle takes its familiar shape. I yearn for the veils to return, but they have passed on, like clouds.

I drag myself to the window. Bushes smother one another, but the gums stand separate and connect only high up in the pale shadows, and sometimes not even then. The ground is a graveyard of autumn leaves. I can make out the swing. Nelum's swing with its green cords and brown wooden seat, dry leaves upon it.

Now the light shines through and there is the child on the swing. Splash of red swinging through green, and a voice rippling the silence. Now a song and breathless laughter spilling over the shade where I sit with my son. She goes too high, then even higher. When she has had enough she swiftly forces the swing to her will and jumps out. She runs up to me, her skin cold and exuberant. I rub her little body to warm her. She is impatient. She pulls at her brother, leaves him, rushes away, shouts something over her shoulder. He draws back against my knees. I weave my fingers through his curly hair. Like a perfumed araliya in a dream, the memory floats.

I pull down the shutter.

Acknowledgements

This novel was written with the assistance of an Individual Writer's Grant awarded by the Government of South Australia through Arts South Australia.

An extract was published under the title 'Mohini' in *Navasilu: Journal of the English Association of Sri Lanka*, vols 15 and 16, English Association of Sri Lanka, Colombo, 1998.

About the Author

Chandani Lokugé has published 15 books. She commenced her writing career with *Moth and other stories*. While continuing to anthologize her short stories, she has published three novels – *If the moon smiled*, *Turtle nest* and *Softly, as I leave you*, recipient of Sri Lanka's Godage National Literary Award in 2013. The first novel, *If the moon smiled* was shortlisted for the New South Wales Premier's Prize. Her fiction has been translated into Greek, French and Hindi, and read on ABC Radio National. As Editor of the *Oxford Classics Series* she has published 7 critical editions of Indian women's writing in English. Among her co-edited special issues of journals are *Journal of Postcolonial Writing*, *Moving Worlds*, *New Literatures Review* and *Meanjin*. A former Australian Commonwealth Scholar from Sri Lanka she is currently Associate Professor of Literary Studies and Creative Writing at Monash University, Australia.